SU
SHREDDER

Breaking the Green

VIVIAN RICHARDSON

Bloomsbury

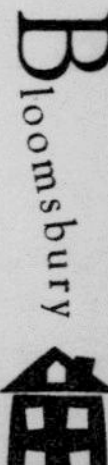

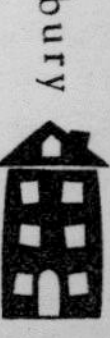

Confused by the surfing jargon?
There's a great glossary at the back!

To Janie

First published in Great Britain in 1996
Bloomsbury Publishing Plc, 2 Soho Square, London W1V 6HB

The moral right of the author has been asserted
A CIP catalogue record of this book is available from the British Library

ISBN 0 7475 2528 5

Cover designed by Alison Withey
Cover illustration by David Wyatt

Typeset by Dorchester Typesetting Group Ltd

Printed by Cox and Wyman Ltd, Reading, Berkshire

10 9 8 7 6 5 4 3 2 1

It was too weird. Jim could not explain it. And it wasn't funny any more.

He was scared. Scared of closing his eyes. Of falling asleep. But most of all, scared of waking. Waking in the early hours to find his bed soaking wet and full of sand, and his pillow wreathed in seaweed again.

He could not hide it from his mum much longer. She was already suspicious. She had noticed the pile of seaweed below his bedroom window, and he had overheard her talking to Russ.

'He's up to something,' she said. 'I can always tell.'

She had special radar when it came to trouble.

'Maybe the kid has heard something,' Russ said. 'You know what they're like – ears always flapping.'

So Jim lay in bed, eyes as wide as they would stretch, staring into the gloom. Wondering.

Through his window he could see the lighthouse on Gunver Point. Its pencil beam sweeping across the dark water of Covin Bay. With each turn the light slanted through his window and fell on the wall where his surfing posters had been.

He had ripped them all down. Every precious one. Scrumpling the waves and creasing the faces of his heroes. He had shoved them into drawers and under his bed in the hope that the dreams would stop if he was no longer surrounded by them all. But it changed nothing.

'I'll never sleep ever again,' he swore.

But he could not fight it forever.

Jim watches the wave rise up out of the deep until he thinks it will wash the grey out of the very sky itself. Sparkling green. Beautiful. Terrible. And in its roar he hears the dying breath of some great distant storm.

'Don't do it, Jimbo! It'll wipe you out!' he hears Danny's warning shout.

The others split in all directions, arms flaying the water as they lie flat on their boards and paddle for safety. Some towards the beach. Others towards the shoulder where the break will be smaller. He stays.

'Jim's going to ride the Twisted Cat!' Danny is shouting over and over.

His every instinct tells him to bail out. Dive. Let the wave roll over him. But his body seems gripped by a force far greater than his own.

He turns to make his run. Lying with his belly flat to the board, he paddles, arm over arm, stroking through the water. Picking up speed as the wave scoops him up, hurling him forward. He moves instinctively, gripping the rails and jumping up. His feet slap on the deck and he takes the drop. It feels as if he has stepped off the edge of the world.

Next, he is lying in the shallows like a piece of driftwood. A hot sun is burning his bare back and legs. The sand gleams like silver.

He scrambles to his knees. He is naked. The wave has stripped him bare. He crouches in the hot sand, covering up as best he can with his hands, face burning red.

'Help! Please! I need some shorts,' he calls to the sunbathers on the beach.

They do not hear him. They do not see him.

He sees the point of a broken surfboard stuck in the sand. It leans, short-shadowed and slanting, a plastic gravestone in the midday sun. He crab-crawls closer, still covering up. He can see strange patterns twisting across the flat of the board, and a face in the sand.

A nose. Cheeks. Chin. A boy's face, sculpted in silver. Lying there, sleeping. Suddenly the eyes flick open and stare at him. Dark eyes. And gradually, the boy rises up out of the sand.

'Who are you? What do you want?' Jim shouts.

'Help Bono. Help Bono,' the sand boy says.

And suddenly the name of a boy he has never even met is as familiar as his own. As if their lives have always been mixed and as intertwined as the snaking signs which cover the broken board. Tied to one another. Beyond all hope. Even beyond the grave.

'. . . NO!' Jim came awake with a start.

He sat up in the darkness of his room, his heart thumping fit to burst out of his chest.

It was a dream. Just a stupid dream. Not real. He tried to shake the memory of it from his head.

But then he felt the dampness in his sheets and the grittiness of the sand between his toes. Trembling, he reached out and switched on the light, and stared at the broken point of the surfboard which lay on the end of his bed.

2

By the time the cartoons had started on Saturday Morning TV, Jim had a plan. It was not his best ever. In fact, just the thought of what he was going to do sent a shiver running through him. But he did not have a better one.

He knew his mum would never let him go, so he thought it best not to ask. After all, what she didn't know couldn't worry her, now could it? That's why he was sneaking out before breakfast with his school pack on his back.

'You're up early, love,' a voice called, as he crept past the open kitchen door.

'Mum. It's you!'

'Who did you expect – Madonna?'

He poked his head round the door. 'Is she staying?'

His mum smiled and shook her head. 'Never mind. Where are you going anyway?'

His stomach tied itself in a knot. She might have been sitting in her dressing-gown and curlers, drinking cups of tea, but he could tell her radar was switched on.

'Nowhere.'

'That's nice – and so early, too.'

They weren't really yellow curlers rolled up in her fringe. They were high tech mind-reading devices, stuffed full of the latest micro chips, which bleeped every time he told a lie.

'I mean Danny's,' he said quickly.

She seemed pleased he had made up his mind, but she was not finished yet.

'And what have you got in that pack?' she asked.

That proved it. She had X-ray eyes, too. Eyes which could see through doors and walls and even people in red sweat-shirts. How else could she have known what he had on his back.

'Nothing,' he said, proving beyond all doubt that it was definitely something interesting.

She made him come in and put the pack on the table. He stood in front of her, shuffling his feet, conscious of the lace missing from his left trainer and the rip in his jeans which he hadn't told her about. He picked nervously at the sleeve of his sweat-shirt and waited.

'You don't have to show me if you don't want to,' she said, breaking the silence.

He sighed. That always meant he did.

'OK. But you won't like it,' he said, pulling at the buckle.

'Then it's more junk from the beach, isn't it?' she said, before he could get the bag open. 'Another dead crab or some horrible, dirty thing to stink out the place – and don't try that "I found it washed up so it must be clean" thing again. It doesn't work on me. So just you get it out of my kitchen!'

'No, I didn't find it on the beach—'

'And I suppose you're going to tell me it flew here in the middle of the night and you found it on the end of your bed?'

He looked at her in amazement. 'How did you know!'

She gave him one of her *disappointed* looks. Like the one she had given him when he had accidentally burnt down the shed and lied about that freak shower of red-hot meteorites which had struck so unexpectedly.

'Sometimes I wonder about you, James

Troon,' she said, with a big, sad sigh. 'Why can't you be like other kids.' She thought for a moment, then her face brightened as if she had had a good idea. 'You could take up a nice hobby – ori-thingy maybe like that nice Charles what's-his-name at school. He makes beautiful things out of paper for his mum.'

'Origami, and Charles Munty isn't nice. He's a twonker,' Jim muttered, unwisely.

That's when it happened. That's when she lost her cool and let it slip.

'I blame those surfie friends of yours. They're a bad influence on you,' she said, her face flushing an angry pink. 'It won't be a bad thing if we do move . . .'

Her voice trailed away, leaving it half said as only a grown-up can.

And suddenly the backpack was forgotten.

'What do you mean *move*?' he asked after a long pause.

'Never mind – just eat your breakfast,' she said, piling Weetos into a bowl.

She made him spoon up every last one, then snatched away his plate and plunged it into the sink. Her knuckles were white as she gripped the scrubbing brush. *Scrutsh*, *scrutsh*, *scrutsh*, the nylon bristles went. Round and round, as if she was trying to remove the willow pattern itself.

She was treating him like a kid again and he wished she wouldn't. He was nearly thirteen. He had eyes. He had ears.

'Russ is coming over later, for a very special tea,' she said. 'We've lots to talk about. The three of us. You know – *later*.'

Suddenly that little word seemed to toll like a cracked bell.

He found it easy to escape after that. Almost too easy. She seemed only too happy to get him out of the house and over to Danny's.

Outside, he settled the pack on his back and turned the brim of his Swordfish cap backwards so it would not blow off. But as he wheeled his bike out of the garage he had the strangest feeling. The feeling that everything in his life had already been decided. In secret. By someone else. And he couldn't help wondering if that someone else was a boy called Bono.

It wasn't all a lie. He *did* go round to Danny's house. He just didn't stay, that's all.

But Jim couldn't help feeling bad as they doubled-back past his house and he caught a glimpse of his mum through the kitchen window. He kept his head low. His bike in high gear. Pumping the pedals as fast as he could until he was round the corner and out of sight.

'Where are we going?' Danny asked, as they reached the main road.

'You'll see.'

'I told my mum we're going down to Wrecker's to watch Sean practise for the North Shore,' Danny said, referring to his big brother and the major surfing competition that weekend. 'She'll bounce off the walls if she discovers we didn't go.'

'Don't worry – we'll go along the coast road,' Jim said. 'Show our faces, then sneak away.

That way everyone is happy.'

A grin split Danny's face. 'You should have seen Sean. He was really choked when Mum told him he had to look after us. Said he was going to set Big Mungo on us.'

'Hope not,' Jim said. 'He doesn't like me.'

'Big Mungo doesn't like anyone,' Danny said, his eyes flicking to the pack on Jim's back. 'Can I have a look?'

'Only if you swear you'll come with me – that you won't chicken out.'

Danny was immediately suspicious. He sat pulling at the spikes of ginger hair which stuck out from underneath his fibreglass helmet. But his curiosity got the better of him. 'OK, I swear.'

'On a dog's head?' Jim said.

Danny nodded. 'On a dog's head.'

'Then I'll show you when we get where we're going,' Jim said and turned down the hill towards the harbour.

'That's not fair!' Danny called, racing after him.

Just outside Porth Covin, around the point where the jumble of the town ended, lay Wrecker's Reef. Facing north-west. Stretched between Covin Bay and the lighthouse on Gunver Point. The huge pinky-grey slabs of granite lurked beneath the waves. The same deadly reef where many storm-driven ships had foundered, lured on to the rocks by the lights of the wreckers.

Jim crested the hill first, and suddenly the little bay was spread before them in the September sunshine. The waves were marching in orderly ranks, uniformed in blue and green with plumes of spuming foam.

'They must be almost one-and-a-half metres and pumping,' he said, and whistled.

Almost two centuries had passed since those wild, unruly men had met with lantern lights and dark purposes. The sea had long since swallowed the wrecks and buried the bleached bones of their victims. Now, only the name remained, marking one of the best left-handed breaks in Cornwall.

Sean was waiting for them in the lay-by at the side of the road. He was wearing his Wave Rider wetsuit – rubber coated from ankles to neck to wrists. He had slicked his blond hair back with gel.

'I'm going to make you suffer for this,' he hissed. 'It doesn't do my image much good to be playing nursemaid to a couple of snotty kids, you know!'

'We won't cause you any trouble, Sean – I promise,' Danny said.

'We just want to watch,' Jim lied.

Sean puffed up with his own self-importance. 'Yeah, well, maybe you'll learn something,' he said. 'But remember, while I'm out there being radical, Big Mungo will be right here watching *you*.'

The mountain with the dreadlocks which was Big Mungo grinned at them and cracked his knuckles.

'Sorry, Jim,' Danny whispered, as they fitted the locks to the wheels of their bikes. 'I thought he was joking about Big Mungo.'

Sean led the way down on to the beach to a spot near the water's edge. There he made them sit down while he traced out a wonky circle around them in the damp sand with a stick.

'You'll be safe in there,' Sean said, looking pleased with himself.

Danny was puzzled. 'How do you mean – safe?'

'It's like this,' Sean explained, 'I promised Big Mungo all the multi-decker burgers he can eat if he makes sure you two stay *inside* that circle.'

'And if we don't?' Jim asked.

Sean screwed up his face as if just the thought of it was painful.

'My advice to you is *never* get between Big Mungo and a multi-decker with extra mayo, cheese and pickle. It's messy – very messy,' he said, then as an afterthought he added, 'Oh and by the way – I told him you two are paying.'

And suddenly Sean's scheme didn't so much whiff of revenge – it *stank*. With only a few coins between them, they were fish food either way. If they made a run for it, Big Mungo would not be very happy about losing his multi-deckers; but it would be worse if they stayed until he found out they did not have any money anyway.

Sean grinned hugely, tucked his buttered board under his arm and ran down to the water's edge. He knelt to attach his ankle rope then slipped easily into the water. They watched as he lay flat on his board and paddled out through the chop towards the line-up.

'Now what are we going to do?' Danny asked, glancing at the dreadlocked mountain of doom sitting close by.

Big Mungo rumbled threateningly. Volcanic.

'I'm thinking,' Jim said.

For a while, he watched Sean sliding effortlessly across curling waves. One after another, dropping into the pocket, picking up speed, cutting back to the lip and floating off the peak, kicking up great fans of light-spangled water. He made it look so easy. As if he was walking on water.

Jim was just wishing he was as good, when he noticed Big Mungo staring. Not at Danny. Not at him. But at the pack on his back. Worse still, Big Mungo was muttering something about food.

'What have you got in there?' Big Mungo said.

'Nothing,' Jim said, again proving beyond all doubt that there was definitely something interesting.

Big Mungo's eyes disappeared into suspicious little slits. He eased himself up off the sand and stood peering out between the twisting tails of hair which dropped over his face.

Then, with surprising speed, he made a grab for the pack. Lifting Jim high off the sand, so he hung in the straps, feet kicking air. Big Mungo tried to shake him off. This way. That. Twisting. Turning. Forward. Back. Rumbling, a boiler about to blow.

'Give it to him!' Danny pleaded.

'I would if I could . . .' Jim said, bouncing about in a raggy sort of way.

Then with a twang the buckle burst and the nose of the broken surfboard popped into the air. It fell on to the sand at their feet and lay there, twitching. Big Mungo frowned, looked inside the empty pack, sniffed and threw Jim away in disgust. He picked up the broken piece of plastic and studied the strange markings. They could all see it was glowing.

Electric blue sparks crackled and buzzed

along the patterns which swirled across the glassy surface. Big Mungo blinked stupidly as the electricity danced around his fingers and set the hairs of his forearms on end. It traced a path all the way to his shoulders.

And suddenly: PZAT-TZOOW! his dreadlocks were standing straight up on his head, pointing at the sky, frizzled and smoking.

'My 'air! My 'air!' he shrieked, dropping the broken board and clamping his big hands to his head.

People were pointing.

'You can keep yer extra pickle,' he shouted, turned and ran blubbering across the sand.

'How did you do that?' Danny said, blinking a lot.

Jim dropped to his knees and picked up the broken piece of board. He slipped it back into his pack. 'I didn't,' he said, buckling the flap. 'It must have been Bono.'

'You must be crazy! I'm not going to Gunver's place!' Danny said, braking hard. His tyres left black marks on the road.

Jim turned his bike in a tight circle in the lane and free-wheeled back to where Danny sat with his arms folded across his chest, unbudgable.

'You promised. You said you wouldn't chicken out,' he said. 'You swore it on a dog's head.'

'Yes, but you didn't say anything about going to see Gunver,' Danny said, nervously eyeing the rough track which led off the lane.

The scraggy hawthorn bushes seemed to close in on either side as if hiding some dark secret. A dead end. It was the only way up to Gunver's place.

Gunver ate cats, everyone knew that. And he could speak fluent crow. And that necklace he wore around his neck was really made of human teeth and fingerbones. And each night he painted himself yellow and danced around a fire of burning skulls to raise the dead. So it was hardly surprising Danny wasn't all that keen to go.

'My mum will go ballistic if he bites off my nose and sucks out all my blood,' he said, miserably. 'And it'll be all your fault, too.'

Gunver wasn't his real name. He didn't seem to have one, at least no one in Porth Covin knew it if he did. He had lived in the lonely cottage out on Gunver Point for so long they just called him Gunver. It seemed as good a name as any to a man who didn't care.

'Lucky he doesn't live out near Stink Beach,' Danny had once joked, referring to the little bay where the old Victorian sewer still drained sewage into the sea.

Exactly seventeen days, three hours and twenty-two minutes later, Danny had tripped over Mrs Milligan's dog and broken a bone in his wrist. Nobody had dared joke about Gunver again after that.

Big-fingered and gaunt, Gunver had wild eyes, a shaven head and a beard which trailed off the point of his chin like whisps of wind-whipped wool. He was more of a prophet of doom than a Shaper who smoothed surf boards for a living.

He only came into Porth Covin once a fortnight to pick up essentials and to sell his brightly painted boards to the Surf Shack. Some said he flew in like a big black crow. Others that he just appeared out of thin air. No one seemed to want to believe he came in the clapped-out, old van Jim had seen him park in the Pay and Display by the church.

'The way I see it,' Jim said, 'if Gunver can raise the dead, he's sure to know why I'm having all these weird dreams. Maybe he can stop them. Or at least tell me who this Bono is. Call him up, or something.'

Danny seemed surprised. 'Do dead people have mobiles, too?'

'Not that kind of call!' Jim said, rolling his eyes. He leant closer as if frightened someone might overhear. 'I reckon Gunver would have to use magic. A 'squeegee' board, maybe, with a glass to spell out the messages from beyond the grave. I've seen it done on TV.' He paused, then added, 'And anyway, have you got a better idea?'

Danny did – plenty – and none of them included going anywhere near Gunver or his boogie boards. But he gave up in the end, as Jim knew he would. He had sworn. On a dog's head.

Soon after they left the road, the track began to climb steeply. It was too rough and rutted for their bikes. So they hid them amongst the bushes and brambles, taking only Jim's pack with them as they continued on foot.

Up, ever up. Twisting their way between the scraggy hedgerows. Jumping at the sound of every kicked stone and startled bird. Until they found their way barred by an old, wooden gate.

Beyond, Gunver's cottage stood silent. Squat beside the barn. The eaves of its slate roof frowning down over salt-weathered stone and cold, dark windows. Here sky and sea and land met, and only a seagull's distant cry scratched at the ear. Here they found true loneliness.

'A witch used to live up here once,' Danny said unhelpfully. 'Mad Meg, they called her. They burnt her at the stake, but some say her ghost still haunts the place.' His eyes grew larger. 'Sometimes you can hear her wailing – like wind on wires, only worse.'

'Who says?'

'Sean swears it's true.'

'And how does Sean know?'

Danny shrugged. 'Just does. So don't go kicking any black cats.' Then, under his breath, 'Mind you, Gunver's probably eaten all of them by now.'

The gate creaked as they climbed over and jumped down on the other side. They picked their way between the bushes of spiky gorse, past Gunver's old orange van, to a window by the front door. Jim rubbed at the blurry glass with his sleeve and peered in.

It was dark inside, but he could see furniture scattered about and shelves bowing with old books. The paint flaked off the walls like butter curls and a single, high-backed chair stood by the fireplace. Empty.

'Too bad he's not home,' Danny said, smiling

for the first time since he had heard Gunver's name that morning. 'We'll just have to come back later – much later. A million years should do.'

Jim ignored him and pressed his ear to the rough wooden door. He was sure he could hear someone moving around inside. He knocked. The door creaked. It was off the latch.

'Are you there, Gunver?' he said. 'It's me – James Troon.'

'And me, Daniel Smith!' Danny added quickly.

'Shhhhhhhhhhhh!' Jim hissed like a broken steam-pipe.

They stood on the doorstep, listening to the wind strumming the wires of the fence and trying not to think of Mad Meg.

'I don't like it, Jimbo,' Danny said. 'Let's split while we can.'

But Jim reckoned they had come too far to turn back now.

He pushed the door and it swung inwards, creaking back on salt-rusted hinges. The cottage smelt warm and sooty, and there was still a glow amongst the crumbling grey ashes in the fireplace.

Suddenly the air was filled with the sound of beating wings and something shiny and black shot out over their heads. They ducked with it swirling in their faces and heard a raucous screech. *Caaaaaaaaaaaaaawwwwwwwwww! Caw! Caw! Caw!*

'Don'd led him ged me!' Danny said, clamping his hand to the end of his nose.

'It was only a crow!' Jim said, his heart pounding.

He caught a glimpse of the big bird as it soared high into the air on purple-black wings. It circled the cottage several times then landed on the roof, caw-cawing its alarm.

But enough was enough for Danny. He let go of his nose just long enough to say that wild, roller-blading elephants could not drag him a step further – promise or no promise – and that he must have been brain-dead bonkers for ever coming in the first place.

'I'm going home,' he said. 'I'm not hanging around here waiting for Mr Nose-biter, Vampire-breath Gunver to turn up.'

But it was too late.

Gunver appeared as if by magic. One moment he was nowhere to be seen, the next he was just standing there. Watching. His long crimson coat flapping around his ankles in the breeze. His arms full of newly-chopped wood.

'The crow told me you had come,' he said, after a long pause.

'Did you hear that!' Danny said. 'The crow told him! The *crow*!'

Gunver's eyes sparkled, and the hint of a smile tugged at the corners of his mouth as if he found something amusing.

'Heard his squawking while I was chopping wood for the fire,' he said, then added, 'Best guard crow I've ever had.'

Jim shifted uneasily in the silence which followed and thought he better say something.

'We, er . . . have come to see you,' he said lamely.

'Guessed that by the way you're knocking on my door.'

'We, I mean, *I* need your help.'

'You had better come in then,' Gunver said.

They stood, hovering uncertainly just inside the open door.

Gunver stacked the wood by the fire then laid several splintered pieces in the grate. He knelt to blow glowing life into the ashes, holding back the long wisps of his goatee beard so they would not singe. The flames soon caught on the dry wood. Pale yellow and weak, at first. Then brighter.

'Tea, then talk,' he said, hanging an old kettle on a wire hook above the flames. He sat back and warmed his hands.

The crow flapped down off the roof and alighted on the doorstep. It cocked its head on one side and fixed them with a beady black eye, then strutted past, head bobbing with each measured step, as solemn as an undertaker come to call. It flapped up to settle on the high back of Gunver's chair and pecked at the horse hair which bulged out of the split leather.

Gunver scratched under its chin. 'He's a good crow, but murder on the furniture,' he said.

And suddenly he was not frightening any more. Tall. Gaunt. Different. But not frightening.

Jim closed the door.

The tea, when it was brewed, tasted good. Hot and sweet, and not in the least bit like the swamp water or frogspawn Danny had been expecting. Only when it had been drunk and the mugs cleared away, was Gunver ready for talk. He sat with the firelight washing and wiping his face, and listened as Jim told him about the dreams.

'Every night it's the same,' he said, and he told Gunver about the giant wave and the strange bay with the silver beach, and of the boy coming out of the sand. 'But worst of all, when I wake up, my bed is wet and full of sand, and there's seaweed on my pillow. Then this morning, I found this —'

He shrugged the pack off his back, lifted the flap and slid out the point of the broken board. Gunver took it and cradled it in his big hands. He studied the markings for a long while, then closed his eyes and sat very still.

'You want to be careful of that thing,' Danny whispered, 'it frizzled Big Mungo's dreadlocks.'

'Wick-id,' Jim said.

Danny shook his head. 'It's the Temple of Doom, more like,' he said.

Once it had been just a barn attached to the cottage, now it was the sacred place where Gunver shaped his boards. Iron sticks held flickering candles, each carrying a dozen or more in their twisted arms, and frozen falls of creamy wax cascaded to the floor. The rough stone walls had been daubed with images of surfers and dolphins and giant, curling waves; stick figures as symbolic as ancient cave paintings. And all around, surfboards stood, points up, like hooded monks waiting in silent attendance.

Gunver was at the long wooden table studying the curling symbols on the broken tip of the board which lay in front of him.

'These signs are part of an equation,' he

said. 'A mathematical equation like you would use at school. The only difference being the signs are very old, like the hieroglyphs you see on the walls of an Egyptian Pharaoh's tomb.'

'What do they mean?' Jim asked.

Gunver's fingers traced over the symbols and his lips moved as if he was reading. One in particular stood out from the rest. A surfer, in profile, with wild hair flying in the wind. The candle-light danced in Gunver's eyes when he finally looked up: 'Would you believe me if I said that you were not dreaming. That you have *been* to this bay with the silver sand?'

'No way! I was in bed. At home all the time,' Jim denied it. 'Anyway, my mum would never let me go.'

'And if I said the sand and seaweed in your bed proves it.'

'It's impossible – isn't it?'

Gunver shook his head. 'Tell me about this boy, the one who comes up out of the sand.'

'I've never seen him before, not ever,' Jim said.

'Not ever?' Gunver's eyes searched his face eagerly.

Jim sighed. 'I know this is going to sound really weird, but . . .'

'. . . You feel as if you know him,' Gunver prompted. 'Despite the fact that you have never even met him?'

Jim was startled. 'Yes.'

Gunver turned to the pile of books on the table and pulled out a heavy, leather-bound volume with SURFING THE TIME NET printed in silver on the spine. He spoke as he flicked through the pages.

'For many years people have dreamt of being able to travel in time,' he said. 'But the amount of energy required for someone to make a quantum leap from one place to another is enormous. Even if we could make a machine which could travel at the speed of light, the forces generated inside it would be too great for our human bodies. So it would be impossible for us to travel faster than Time, unless . . .' He shook his head as if he could hardly believe it himself, '. . . unless we could slow down Time itself.'

'Yes, but what has all this got to do with *me*?' Jim asked.

'It means, James Troon, that I think this boy, the one you call Bono, is from the future. *Your* future,' he said. 'And, if I'm right, he has come back to warn you.'

'To warn me? Why? About what?'

'Only he can answer those questions,' Gunver said. 'That is why you must go to him.'

Jim's eyes were as round as CDs. 'Go to him? How?'

'He has shown you the way,' Gunver said, picking up the point of the broken board. 'But first, we have much to do.'

'He's as crazy as bottled pizza,' Danny whispered. 'No way is this going to work.'

'Let's see what happens,' Jim said.

Gunver chose a blank board from amongst the ones in the barn and laid it flat on the table. It was creamy white and brand new. Unshaped.

Jim stepped forward. He felt as if a thousand eyes were on him; as if the rafters, where the shadows jigged and danced at the candles' whim, were filled with silent watchers, waiting to see what he would do.

His hands trembled as he placed the broken piece of board so it covered the nose of the new board beneath.

'Told you it wouldn't work,' Danny said, after what seemed an age of time had passed.

But he was wrong.

It began as a faint glow and grew brighter. Before long, crackling blue sparks were tracing along the twisting patterns on the tip of the broken board and on to the pale, blank beneath. Slowly the broken piece and the new board began to merge, dissolving into a mist of coloured lights which swirled before their eyes. And gradually the barn filled with a deep, throbbing hum.

'Nice one, Jimbo,' Danny groaned, backing away.

Then they heard a rushing sound, like wind blowing down a long tunnel. It grew steadily louder until it was a roar.

'Watch out!' Gunver said.

The blast, when it came, blew all the candles out and knocked Jim off his feet. He went sliding across the floor and came up against the wall with a thump. He struggled to his knees, the wind whipping his face, and caught hold of Danny as he went spinning past. But as suddenly as it had come, the wind was gone, leaving them dishevelled and breathless.

'It is done,' Gunver said, breaking the silence.

'Please don't make me come with you next time, Jimbo,' Danny begged as they stood up.

But Jim was too busy staring at the new board lying on the table to pay much attention. The old broken point and new board had fused together to become one.

'Awesome,' he said, breathlessly.

And awesome it was. Like no board he had ever seen. Built for speed and manœuvrability, narrow and yet beautifully balanced. A little over two metres from pointed nose to crescent tail. With mystical markings and strange signs which swirled across it. It curved with the grace of a deep-sea fish.

'What a surf shredder,' he said, running his

fingers down the smoothness of its line. He felt the sharp pin-prick of electricity. 'Is it really for me?'

Gunver nodded. 'I have heard many surfers say that time seems to stop inside a tube,' he said. 'Well maybe it really does, just for a split second. Just long enough for the power of this strange board to take you into another *dimension*.'

'Did he mention what?' Danny asked.

'Think he means to another place,' Jim said.

'And time,' Gunver said. 'For if I am right, with this board you will be able to surf on time itself.'

Jim pulled his hand away as if he had touched something hot. The glow faded and he felt cold, as if something precious had been taken from him. He looked longingly at the board, but shook his head.

'My mum wouldn't like *that*,' he said. 'And anyway, I don't know what to do – how to use it.'

'You have been shown the way,' Gunver said.

Jim frowned and thought for a moment, then he went very pale. 'The monster wave?'

Gunver nodded.

'But we don't get surf that big in Cornwall,' Danny said, 'apart from the . . .' His voice trailed away.

'The Twisted Cat,' Gunver said. 'Yes, James Troon. The boy you call Bono wants you to ride the Twisted Cat.'

6

Later.

His mum had cooked burgers and chips for tea. Spread the best table cloth. Folded paper napkins. And when Russ arrived bang on five o'clock wearing a tie, Jim knew that something was up for sure.

They sat in silence except for a polite, 'Please may I have the ketchup,' every now and again. Nervous glances ricocheting around the table.

'Are you going to marry my mum?' Jim asked Russ at last.

He could tell he had caught them by surprise.

'Well, that's what we wanted to talk to you about, love,' his mum said quickly. She shot a pleading look at Russ.

Russ tugged at his tie as if it was strangling him. 'You see, it's like this, mate—' he started to explain.

'Does that mean we'll have to live in Australia?' Jim interrupted.

The big Aussie paused, then nodded. 'I've finished my research here and I'm being transferred back home, to a place called Whaler's Bay,' he said. 'They want me to set up a marine biology lab down there.'

'But what about Danny? What about school?'

'You would have a new school and make plenty of new friends, love,' his mum said. 'And who knows, Danny might be able to come and stay with us.'

Jim nodded, but he knew Australia was a long way away. He liked Russ and he wanted his mum to be happy, but the thought of leaving Porth Covin made him sad. How could he ever be happy anywhere else?

'Think I'll go up my room now,' he said, when they had cleared away the dishes. He felt their eyes following him and he turned to Russ. 'It's OK, you know,' he said. 'As long as you promise never to go and leave us like my dad did.'

'I promise, mate,' Russ said.

'On a dog's head?' Jim asked.

'On a dog's head.'

Jim stood at his window and looked out over the jostling roofs of Porth Covin, across Covin Bay towards the lighthouse on the far-flung rocks of Gunver Point. Wrecker's Reef lay hidden from view by the Point in between, but he knew the best surfers would still be surfing the incoming tide. Waiting for the Twisted Cat.

Mr Starling had spent a whole Geography lesson explaining: 'Tourists come from all over to see it,' he had said. 'But there is nothing very unusual about the wave apart from its size. You see, it's a tidal bore.'

'So it's not very interesting, then,' Danny had called from the back.

They had laughed at that.

But exactly seventeen pages, three paragraphs and twenty-two lines of extra homework later, no one was laughing at Mr Starling any more.

He had drawn diagrams in chalk on the board. 'A tidal bore is formed when the incoming floodtide meets the opposing currents and the water is forced into the steeply-shelving bay. The result is a spectacular and dangerous surge of water which takes the form of the plunging wave we can see each evening at about six thirty p.m.'

'Why is it called the Twisted Cat?' someone had asked.

'Because it's mean and twisty and the rip can claw you under,' Danny had piped up, but he noticed the dangerous look in Mr Starling's eyes and had shut up.

Jim thought about the board hidden behind the boxes in the garage. He had covered it with an old counterpane. But he knew it wouldn't be long before his mum's radar took her right to it. She would go completely tonto if she found out he had been up to Gunver's house.

There was a gentle knock on the door.

'Are you all right, love?' his mum asked, poking her head in.

'I'm OK,' he said, quickly pulling up the roll-neck of his sweater so she would not see the black rubber of the wetsuit he was wearing underneath.

'Russ likes you very much – you know that, don't you?'

'Yeah.'

'We'll talk about it in the morning,' she said. 'When you've had a chance to think.'

'In the morning,' Jim repeated automatically.

She smiled and closed the door.

He listened for her footsteps on the stairs, slid open the window and climbed out.

He met Danny at the end of his road, secretly as arranged. Then they took the short cut across the fields, running with their boards bouncing under their arms.

The usual bag of diehards were out when they arrived at Wrecker's. Sean was in the line-up, bobbing amongst the waves like a blond seal. Big Mungo was standing at the water's edge waxing his board. The others were mostly spectators.

'Are you really going to do it?' Danny said, panting.

'I have to,' he said, kicking off his shoes and

stripping down to his wetsuit. 'Especially now.'

'Why *especially* now?'

Jim kept his eyes fixed on the line of the break and said nothing. The waves were smaller, but still peeling. Coming in sets of three, rolling in one after another for an even break. It looked innocent enough and yet he knew that out there – somewhere – a monster lurked.

'If it works and I really can travel in time, then it wouldn't matter where I lived, would it?' he said.

Danny looked puzzled and supposed not. Then his face brightened as if he had just had an idea. 'If it works, then maybe you could find out the winning numbers in next week's lottery.'

Jim grinned and pulled on the long tab of his zipper, drawing it up his back to the nape of his neck. Picked up the board and ran to the water's edge. He knelt to attach the plastic leash to his ankle. The far-flung ripples of a dying wave sucked at his knee, then slid back slowly with a disappointed hiss.

The board came alive as soon as it touched the cold water. Buzzing beneath him as he paddled out. Slicing through the chop effortlessly. He went duck-diving as the waves broke over him. Until he reached the line-up.

The Vets were out – the select group of surfers who rode the Twisted Cat regularly – sitting astride their boards in the line-up, waiting. Jim was met by gnarly stares as he joined them.

'No grommets!' they called.

'Take your crazy new stick and clear off, kid – before the Big Cat eats you.'

The Twisted Cat seemed the least of his worries. He would have caught the next wave all the way in had he not noticed the scratch of crimson against the grey.

Gunver was standing on the cliffs near Gunver Point. His bright coat contrasting with the evening sky. His arms raised. A black speck lifted into the air from one outstretched hand, and headed out to sea. It was the crow. The bird flew on, dwindling in the distance.

Jim pulled the nose of his board into a tight turn and chased a small wave. As he picked up speed he gripped the rails and felt the same tingling buzz running through him. But he mis-timed the jump and slid off the back. The wave rolled on.

Maybe the board's not so special, he thought

as he paddled back.

Shivering, he sat astride his board and rode the bucking swell. He let the next set roll under him. A good set of three followed, the waves marching in one after the other, tall and erect. He let the first pass. Then turned to make his run.

The wave bumped up to about head height and he felt the board kick forward. The tingling buzz ran though him and suddenly he could do no wrong. His toes tapped in and he dropped into the pocket easily. He found the sweet spot as if it had been marked with a sign. Laughing, he cut back and kicked into a turn which even a Vet would have been proud of.

'Radical move, man!' someone shouted as he paddled back to the line-up.

He was so pleased, he almost turned neon. But the inner glow quickly faded when he saw Sean paddling towards him.

'What are you doing out!' Sean hissed.

'Just catching waves,' Jim said, not wanting to let on.

'Well, you shouldn't be – not with the Cat coming,' Sean said, and a scared look came into his eyes. 'Danny isn't out too, is he?'

Jim shook his head quickly. 'I left him on the beach.'

But Danny *was*. He was half-way out, ducking through the waves, paddling towards them.

'You crazy grommets!' Sean said. 'The Cat's too big – you'll get hammered.'

Then he saw it.

Jim watched the wave rise up out of the deep until he thought it would wash the grey out of the very sky itself. Sparkling green. Beautiful. Terrible. He saw it trip on the shallows, sucking up sand and seaweed to cloud and beard its face.

'Don't do it, Jimbo!' he heard Danny shout.

The others split in all directions, arms flaying the water as they lay flat on their boards and paddled. Some towards the safety of the beach. Others towards the shoulder where the break would be smaller. He stayed with the Vets in the impact zone.

'Jim's going to ride the Twisted Cat!' Danny was shouting over and over to Sean.

Jim's every instinct told him to bail out. Dive. Let the wave roll over him. But his body seemed gripped by a force far greater than his own.

He turned to make his run. Stroking

through the water. He felt the power of the wave sucking at his board. He moved instinctively, gripping the rails and jumping up. His feet slapped on the deck and he dropped off the edge of the world.

He hit the face of the wave about half-way down and swooped into the pocket to make his turn. Digging in the inside rail, he pushed hard with his back foot and brought the nose smoothly into the turn. Suddenly he was slashing across the wave shooting white water like rocket fire.

A lifetime seemed captured in that moment with the wave curling in over his head. A second? An hour? A year? Time suddenly had no meaning. He stood frozen inside the tube. A statue.

His body was glowing with the strange light. He stared as his hands began to disappear. Soon his arms had vanished. His legs too. The wave was exploding all around him. The green turned to silver and the mouth of the shining tube began to close. Then at the last moment, a blast of air blew him out like a pea, far out into the blue.

Travelling in time was easy. It was ending up lost with no clothes on which was difficult.

Jim shot out of the tube into the blue of a summer's day. The board took him up to the lip, hit the white water and slipped him sideways. He usually fell off when he tried a floating turn, but this time his feet seemed glued to the deck. Down, he swooped, deep into the trough, and rode the wave all the way in before realising he was totally skins.

He hit the water fast and came up in the shallows like a piece of driftwood. The sun was

hot on his bare back and legs. The sand gleamed like silver.

I must be dreaming again, he thought.

The beach was so familiar. A crescent of white sand pinched between rocky points. Beyond the dunes, the land sloped steeply, camouflaged with bushes of boobialla and spiny wattle. At the very top an angled tin roof glinted in the sun.

'Help! Please! I need some shorts,' he called to some sunbathers nearby.

But the roar of the ocean pummelled his words and the wind whipped them away uselessly.

He scrambled to his knees, crouching on the hot sand and covering up as best he could. Face burning red.

Then a thought popped into his head. If it was only a dream, then there was no need to worry. They could not hear him. They could not see him.

'Clothes don't matter in dreams!' he shouted, standing up. He laughed and started prancing about and kicking up sand.

But something was wrong. He stopped prancing and frowned. If he was dreaming again, where was the board stuck in the sand.

Where was the boy? And, more importantly, why were all those people pointing at him, laughing?

Then he remembered the Twisted Cat and it clicked. The full naked truth of it.

Jim would have made the twenty-metre dash from the water's edge to the safety of the dunes easily, had he not forgotten the board attached to his ankle. The plastic leash tripped him neatly. Sent him sprawling. Face down. SPLAT! on to the wet sand. He struggled to his knees. Everyone was laughing now.

He used the board to cover up and waddled up the sand like a lost penguin. Someone started clapping and the others picked it up. He wished the ground would swallow him with every step. He reached the dunes and disappeared into the thickest bush he could find.

Gunver had been right. It had worked. The strange power of the board had taken him to another place as easily as if he had crossed the road. Where, he did not know, but judging by the deep blue of the sky and the burning heat of the sun he was a long way from home. But what was he to do now? And how was he going to do it if he was lost, alone and as naked as the day he was born.

'Why did I do it!' he groaned. 'I'm so stupid! Stupid! Stupid! Stupid!'

The tears burnt the backs of his eyes. They welled up and ran down, leaving pink trails in the salt crusting on his cheeks. He buried his face in his hands and gave in to his despair, his whole body racked by great, gulping sobs.

'Are you all right?' a voice said unexpectedly.

Startled, he crouched low like a hunted animal gone to ground. Through the leaves he could see a girl.

Please don't let her see me, he thought. Not like this. Please. Pleeeeeeeeease.

'I know you're in there,' she said. 'I brought you a towel.'

He heard rustling as something orange and stripy was pushed into the undergrowth. Then nothing. Expecting a trick, he stayed very still, frightened of giving himself away. The minutes stretched. Still nothing happened. He reached out and pulled the towel in, wrapping it around his waist as quickly as he could.

At first, he thought she had gone. It was not until he had pushed out of the bush backwards, pulling his board after him, that he noticed her white T-shirt. She was sitting on the top of a sand dune, hugging her knees and staring out to sea. Her long sandy hair blowing over her shoulders, flicking in the wind like sedge grass.

'Thanks – for the towel,' he mumbled.

'Reckoned you would have stayed in there forever otherwise,' she said, without looking round. 'Least until the snakes got you.'

'Snakes!'

She nodded and looked serious. 'Andy says he saw a Tiger round here last week.'

'Are there tigers, too?' Jim said, peering into the bushes. It sounded as if he had had a lucky escape.

The girl laughed, her green eyes sparkling. 'Where are you from?' she asked, but before he could answer she said, 'I know, you're the new kid. I've seen you at school.'

'You have?'

She nodded. 'My name's Fiona Finn, but everyone calls me Finny.'

'Jim Troon.'

'Then you've just moved into the Bonnington's old place,' she said, her gaze scuttling back to the safety of the sea.

'Have I?'

'You don't know much, do you?' she said.

'I'm lost,' he said quickly.

'It's up there,' she said, pointing at the tin

roof they could see shining in the sun. She stood up and brushed the sand off her shorts. 'Come on – I'll show you.'

Jim's head was buzzing as she led the way up the steep path, winding between the scrubby bushes. It was all too weird. Here he was talking to a girl he had never even met and yet she seemed to know everything about him.

'You put on a bit of a show back there,' she said, when they finally reached the narrow road at the top.

Jim blushed a deep pink and mumbled something about losing his shorts.

'I don't mean on the beach – got three stupid brothers, see,' she said, as if prancing around with nothing on was her brothers' favourite pastime. 'I meant on the wave. You were fat.'

'It was nothing,' he said, as if he was always floating off the top of big waves.

'This is it,' she said, stopping at the gate.

The house was single storey and falling down. The neglected garden, brown and dead. And the bright sun made the shadows under the bushes and trees dark and gloomy.

He noticed the uneasy look in her eyes again. They kept darting down the drive towards the house as if she was half-expecting to see someone.

Suddenly a crackling buzz jolted though the board under his arm. He cried out and almost dropped it.

Finny stared at him, her face very pale. He could see goosebumps on her arms and she shivered as if she was very cold.

'I've got to go,' she said, backing away quickly.

'Why? What's wrong?'

'Nothing – I've just remembered I said I'd meet someone at Sharky's place.'

She turned and walked away quickly.

'What about your towel?' Jim called after her, but she did not look back. He watched until she turned the corner. 'She felt it, too,' he murmured.

A crow lifted off the roof and flapped lazily away as Jim stopped to look up at the old house.

The weatherboards were peeling off the walls. The bullnosed veranda sagged, the painted iron lace hanging off it like a frosted fringe. A fly-screen door knocked gently, moving in the wind.

He propped his board against the wall and pushed open the door. A long, narrow passage stretched away in front of him. Cobwebs drifted in the corners and, here and there, he could see unfaded rectangles on the walls where paintings had hung.

'Where have you been, love?' a voice called.

'Mum! Is that you?'

She emerged from a doorway, arms full of odd shapes half-wrapped in newspaper. 'Who did you expect – the Queen of Sheba?'

'No, but . . . well, it's just that . . .' he said, wishing Danny was there to help him explain.

'You promised to help me with the unpacking,' she said, interrupting. 'And who were you were talking to by the gate?'

'Er, Finny,' he said, then added, 'I think.'

She brightened immediately. 'A friend? See. What did I tell you, love. We've only been living in Whaler's Bay for two weeks and you're already making new friends.'

'Whaler's Bay? But that's – in Australia.'

'Of course it is,' she said, then her face fell into a frown. 'Are you all right, love? You're acting very strange.'

He had noticed the photograph tucked in amongst the things she was carrying. The newspaper was falling away. It was a wedding photograph in a silvered frame. Russ and his mum smiling out, shoulders freckled with confetti, and, beside them, his own face staring back at him.

The picture began to swim before his eyes.

Dizzy, he stumbled. He heard his mum calling for Russ. Her voice echoed as if it was coming to him down a long tunnel. He heard the clump of boots on wood. The darkness came creeping into his head and he felt his knees give way, then remembered no more.

'It's probably the heat, poor love,' his mum was saying as he opened his eyes again.

She and Russ were talking outside his door.

'I warned him about the sun,' Russ said. 'He should have been wearing a hat.'

Jim sat up in bed and looked around his bedroom. He knew it was *his* because his things were spilling out of the boxes everywhere, half unpacked. His scrumpled surfing posters were pinned to the wall, too. And his Jurassic dino-clock was on the bedside table. A Tyrannosaurus Rex with glowing eyes and a prehistoric roar for an alarm, eating time.

Time! The time and date were on the liquid crystal screen: 11.20 a.m., 20:3.

'That's the 20th of March,' he said.

Months had passed since he had taken the drop on the Twisted Cat. Now it was summer and he was living in Australia. His whole life had changed.

So that's how Finny knew so much about me, he thought.

He slipped out of bed and opened the window. The breeze brought scents off the land, reminding him of honey and digestive biscuits, and of how hungry he had suddenly become. Below his window, in the near distance he could see the tussocky dunes and the curving crescent of the beach. Beyond, the blue of the ocean spread out before him endlessly.

It was scary to think he was in another place. In another time during his own life. He could hardly believe it, but it was true. It had *happened*. And to him – James Troon.

He didn't know why he had been called there. Or what he was supposed to do now. But the fear in Finny's eyes had proved one thing. Whaler's Bay had a secret. A dark secret. And somehow he knew Bono was part of it.

'Where are you, Bono?' he said.

The curtains billowed around him and he shivered despite the warm breeze.

'But Mum, I've got to go to Sharky's place,' Jim said. 'It's important.'

'You mean that café on the edge of town?'

He supposed he did. And she supposed it wouldn't harm, if he really was feeling better and he promised to stay out of the sun. She could drop him off, on the way to her Saturday afternoon shop-up at the supermarket.

Jim sat in the front seat and watched the town pass. It reminded him of Porth Covin, nestling in the cup of the bay, but the houses were different. They were flatter and fatter – more modern, with tin roofs instead of slate – and the gardens in front bigger and full of wonderful plants and flowers.

They passed a sign saying WHALER'S BAY WELCOMES YOU and turned down a wide main street of brightly-coloured shops and stores. The buildings all had verandas, and the side-streets had unfamiliar names like Koppamurra, Gawler, and Dream Street. Thoughts carouselled in his head making him dizzy and scared: Was this his home now? Would he ever see Porth Covin again? And what about Danny? What about his friends?

He fought back feelings of rising panic and made himself stay calm. True, it wasn't every day he took the drop on a wave on a grey day at Wrecker's and ended up in a place he had hardly even heard of, but he was there and he couldn't change it. He had to stay calm or he would lose it.

I wish Danny was here to help me, he thought.

While Jim was thinking, the car came to a stop in the main square. A band was playing marching tunes and a crowd had gathered in front of a platform. Above, strung between two poles, a long banner moved in the breeze. The words, VOTE FOR MORGAN GRIST – BUSINESS WORKING FOR THE ENVIRONMENT, were emblazoned on it.

A big man wearing a pale blue suit and white shoes was addressing the crowd: 'For those *few* people who don't know me, my name is Morgan Grist of Morgan Grist Chemicals,' he said, attempting to smooth the few remaining strands of his hair over his bald patch.

His secretary clapped loudly, then continued jotting notes on her pad.

'As you know, we at Morgan Grist Chemicals have always put the environment before our profits . . .' his speech started and went on, '. . . and while I know some of the more radical members of the surfing community disagree,' his voice grew harsher. 'I would like to remind everyone that without chemical plants such as my own there would be no plastics.' He paused to let his words sink in, then finished with a flourish, 'And without plastics there would be no *surfboards*!'

His secretary whinnied with laughter and clapped even louder.

As their car moved on, Jim looked for Finny's face amongst the crowd. But she wasn't there.

Sharky's place turned out to be an old shack on the sea front. A café, which squatted amongst the sand dunes and reminded Jim of a ship-wreck. The wooden walls had been washed out by time and the salt had rusted holes in the corrugated roof. The jaws of a Great White were nailed over the door, spread wide like a trap, and a fishing net looped between a broken post and the piles of assorted junk.

'I'll be back in an hour,' his mum said, and made him promise to be there. 'You'll be grounded for life if you're not.'

A strong smell of chips wafted out of the open door, and everyone turned to look as Jim walked in.

'You wanna milkshake, kid? Chocolato? Strawberry? I gotta everyting,' the big man polishing the counter said, in an accent you could peel like an Italian onion.

His belly hung in his dirty string vest like a big, bloated fish, and his straggling black hair was tied back in a pony tail. He had a big moustache. A pet crow, on a perch, just like Gunver's. And the sign on the wall claimed he served the best doughnuts in town. This was the legend, better known as Sharky.

Jim shook his head. 'I'm looking for someone – a girl called Finny.'

Sharky rolled his eyes, muttered something about living on air, and flapped his rag towards a table in the corner by the window.

'You're new here, aren't you?' a cool-looking kid with curly hair said, coming up beside him unexpectedly. When Jim nodded and introduced himself, he smiled and bought six cans of coke.

'*Him* – I like,' Sharky said, happy again.

'My name's Pete, but everyone calls me Spinner,' he said. 'And you are just in time.'

'In time for what?' Jim asked.

Spinner just grinned and gathered up the cans. He led the way to a table by the window and put the cans down.

'That's Andy Tan,' he said, nodding to a dark-haired boy who was sitting in the corner. 'He's from China, but he lives here now. He can speak Tangerine.'

'Mandarin,' Andy hissed.

Spinner ignored him and pointed to a girl with red hair and ears studded with earrings. 'Sal – she's pretty cool, for a girl.'

'I can beat Spin on to a wave any day,' she said, leaning back in her chair casually.

'That's Tango.' Spinner introduced the wiry kid with the cap turned backwards who was sitting next to Sal.

'Slammed, man. Rap the tuna,' he said.

No one seemed to know what language he spoke.

The next chair was empty.

'Finny had to go suddenly,' Sal explained.

Spinner frowned. 'She's been acting real strange all day,' he said. 'Well, we'll just have to play Canon Head without her.'

He picked out one of the cans and held it up so everyone could see. They all nodded solemnly. He shook it violently and passed it to Andy who did the same. And so on, round the circle. Each shaking it in turn. Until there was little doubt that it would explode if it was opened.

When the can reached Spinner again he put it on the table with the others. Then he mixed them up, switching the cans around, this way and that, until no one knew which one was which.

'You all know the rules,' Spinner said, without bothering to explain them to Jim.

Andy chose first. His fingers playing across each of the six cans in turn until he settled on one.

'Can on head! Canon head! Canon head!' the others began to chant.

Andy put the can on his head. Holding it firmly, he hooked his finger under the ring-pull. He pulled: *Pffffst!* A tiny trail of gas escaped.

Sal's turn. She chose without hesitation. She just reached out, picked a can and put it on her head. A moment later she pulled the tab: *Pffffst!*

The odds were getting worse: a one in four chance of picking the bomb.

Tango's hand hovered, first over one can, then another, until finally he chose.

They watched, eyes glittering, as he made a big show of placing it on his head. Balancing it delicately, his pinky finger extended as if he was having tea with the Queen. He hooked a finger under the tab, smiling so much his face almost split in two.

'Canon head! Canon head!'

Pffffst!

Tango was so disappointed he wanted another go. 'My turn next!' Spinner said, even though it wasn't. He had snatched up a can before Jim even knew what was happening. The sweat gleamed on his forehead. His eyes darted around the table, daring anyone to try and stop him.

'Canon head! Canon head!' Andy started the chant and the others picked it up.

Spinner put the can on his head. The chant reached fever pitch. He held his breath, and pulled the tab.

Pffffst!

All eyes turned to Jim. Two cans were left out of the six. The odds were 50/50.

'Pick one,' Spinner said quietly.

Jim chose quickly, afraid they would think he was scared if he hesitated too long. He put the can on his head and closed his eyes.

'Pop the tab!' he heard Spinner say.

Jim counted to three and pulled.

The noise was terrific. A great crash, followed by a loud bang which had them all half out of their skins. It was so loud no one heard Jim's can let its fizz go with a gentle hiss.

Finny almost took the door off its hinges as she crashed through it, sending it banging back against the wall. She side-stepped a table and came to a sliding halt.

'Mr Grist . . . His car . . . Outside . . . Coming here . . .' she said, panting.

Spinner jumped up. 'Grist! What does he want?'

'Well, well, this is nice,' Mr Grist said, as he stepped in through the door, closely followed by his secretary, writing everything he said down on her note-pad.

The gold frames of his mirrored sunglasses

flashed as he looked around. And when he smiled it was the sort a shark might smile just before it eats you.

'May I remind you, Mr G,' his secretary said, 'that you have an important meeting . . .'

Mr Grist waved her aside. 'Nothing is more important than talking to the little people, Ms Pender,' he said. 'After all, today's kiddies are tomorrow's voters.'

He walked slowly around the café. Every now and again running his finger along the counter or across a table-top, and inspecting his finger-tips.

'It seems', he said, after a long pause, 'I'm to blame for everything? If a surfer has earache or a swimmer an upset stomach, then people start pointing the finger. "Leaks," they say. "Chemicals in the water." ' He struck a dramatic pose, his hand to his forehead. 'It *wounds* me to hear all the vicious rumours about me and my company.'

'I've seen the tears in his eyes,' Ms Pender said.

'That'll be right – crocodile tears,' Spinner whispered.

Mr Grist went on, 'It is my belief that these rumours have been perpetrated—'

'Perper-what?' Sharky asked, looking puzzled.

'. . . *trated.* Oh, never mind!' Mr Grist said. 'It is my belief that these rumours have been spread by people who are frequenting this establishment.'

'Ah, no! N-n-n-n-no!' Sharky said, waggling his finger about in the air. 'That isa too much. No person is frequenting in my establishment!'

Mr Grist pinched the bridge of his nose in a tired sort of fashion. 'What I am trying to say, with some difficulty,' he said, a dangerous tone in his voice, 'is that I want the rumours to stop.'

'They are not helping Mr Grist,' Ms Pender said, 'or his chances of being elected on to the council—'

'Thank you, Ms Pender!' Mr Grist interrupted. He glared her into silence, then continued with a piece of advice. 'The rumours had better stop or I might just tell my friends at the Department of Health about this dirty little hole you call a café. I'm sure they'll agree if there is a hazard to anyone's health, it is to be found here and not out in the bay.' He smiled. 'They are sure to close it down for good.'

'For *bad* more like!' Sharky said.

Ms Pender's calls for three cheers for Mr Grist were greeted by a loud raspberry. Then everyone started shouting: 'No way!' 'Leave Sharky alone!'

'This is our place!'

Mr Grist's triumph was complete and it made Jim boil up inside. He didn't think twice. He just snatched the remaining can from the table and handed it to Mr Grist.

'You must be thirsty after all that, Mr Grist,' he said.

Mr Grist hesitated, smacked his lips, then nodded and took the can. 'That's what I like to see,' he said. 'A bit of respect, where respect is due.' And without another word he swept out.

Ms Pender hurried after him calling, 'You were brilliant, Mr G. Just brilliant. You showed them!'

A moment later and they were all piling out into the bright sunshine, just in time to see Mr Grist slip easily into the back seat of his white limousine. They watched as the smoked-glass window slid up smoothly, masking his smugness.

Silence. A muted *Pop*. Then, *Pffffffffff-sssssssssssssssssssssst!*

'Messy,' Spinner said, grinning. '*Very* messy.'

Two days later, and Jim was surfing with Spinner and the others off Silver Beach.

After Mr Grist's messy 'accident', Jim found himself well-in with everyone; everyone, that is, except Finny who continued to keep her distance.

As Tango put it, he was a 'Chillin', numero uno bonza for making Mr G surf the fizz in his own stretcho.'

Which Jim assumed was good.

Mind you, going to Whaler's Bay High was not so easy. Especially as he was supposed to know his way around. So most of the time he just followed the others, doing what they did, hoping no one would notice. But every now and again, he would look up and catch Finny watching him.

'What happened to Bono?' he had asked Spinner on the way down to the beach after school.

'You mean you don't know?'

'I wouldn't ask if I did.'

'He vanished about a year ago – surfing Coffin.'

'Must have been snorewin, man,' Tango said, shaking his head. 'Lurk outback and a sneaker set is sure to clean you up. Go over the falls at Coffin and they nail the lid.'

Luckily Spinner translated: 'There's this big hole in the reef off Silver. No one knows how deep it is,' he said. 'They say you can see it from planes and stuff. It looks like a coffin. If a wave packs you into that one then you *never* come up.'

'Is that what happened to Bono?'

Spinner had shrugged. 'No one knows for sure. He was out surfing after a storm. They reckon the waves were just too big.'

Jim joined the line-up, and sat astride his board with the waves rolling under him. They were bumping up nicely, but he was letting most of them go. Being careful. He still did not know if he could control the strange powers of the board buzzing beneath him.

Who knows where I might end up, he thought.

'Never seen a stick like that before,' he heard Andy say. 'Those markings look like some weird kind of spell.'

'Maybe it's magic,' Sal suggested.

Spinner passed on the news. 'Hey, Tango! Jim's board does tricks.'

Tango to Finny. 'The Pom's honey does a Merlin,' he said, leaving her none the wiser.

Jim moved away from the main group, but he could feel them watching him and knew they were talking. So he decided to chase a wave just to shut them up. He felt the familiar buzz as he jumped up and kicked in. The board shot forward as if it was turbo-charged, cut back, shredded the lip into a rainbow shower, and was taking him down the face when someone cut across in front of him.

'Watch it!' he yelled, as the board shuddered beneath his feet. He dug the rail in hard. Too late. He lost his balance and plunged head first into the froth.

The wave rolled over him and he popped up behind. He could see the surfer who was responsible for his tumble not far away. A boy, about his age, with long dark hair. Bobbing about in the water.

'It was my wave – you should've kicked off!' Jim called.

The boy just raised a hand and beckoned to him.

Maybe he's hurt, Jim thought, paddling towards him.

A wave bumped up and he ducked through it, but when he came up on the other side he was surprised to find the boy had gone. He sat up on his board and craned his neck to see over the waves. He caught a glimpse of some-one further out.

Again, Jim saw the boy waving. Again, Jim paddled towards him, only to lose him amongst the waves once more.

He shaded his eyes and squinted into the shimmering reflection of the sun on the water. He was almost half-way to the outer break now. The beach was just a blurry line behind him. And he could feel the strong rip of the current sucking at his board, pulling him out where only the sea birds dipped and rose.

'I'm too far out,' he said, stomach knotting.

He made to turn back, but a movement caught his eye. It was the boy again, only now he was right out. Out where the biggest waves were breaking over the outer reef. He seemed so small against the ragged lines of the surf which roared and crashed about him. A curling gash of white rose up and crashed down.

'No!' Jim shouted, as the wave swallowed the boy up.

He flattened himself to the board and paddled, thrashing the water to foam in his hurry to reach the boy. He ducked through the waves and did not stop until he reached the very edge of the outer break. Only then did he see the fins.

There were three of them. Grey. Shining. Rubbery fins, dipping and rising in the water, leaving thin rippling trails behind.

'Sharks!' he gasped, the terror gripping him.

He panicked. Wrenched the nose of his board round and raced straight into the impact zone.

Out there, the waves were like rolling railway embankments. Huge. Unstoppable. With the full weight of the mighty Australian Bight behind them, they tripped on the outer reef and curled in all wind-knotted and uneven.

Jim looked up helplessly as one thundered down on him. Ponderously, inexorably, it closed out. Crashing with the noise of a falling building. Pushing him down with its full weight

Down.

Down.

Down, he went in a tumbling mass of bubbles. Down where only the sun-dappled rocks waited. Round and round, until he lost all sense of time and place. He felt a sharp tug as the leash attached to his leg released and his board speared away. Then he was rolling until he thought he would never stop.

When he opened his eyes he was on the bottom. Above, he could see the water's endless seething tumble, but down there it was strangely calm. He saw a bright light shining, but when he tried to go towards it he found Bono standing in his way.

As transparent as the water around him, Bono shimmered, shot through with shafts of light. His mouth was moving, but no sound came out.

'What is it? What are you trying to tell me?' Jim said, the words bubbling out of his mouth.

Bono held out his hand. A shell was glinting in his palm.

No sooner had Jim's fingers closed around it, than the dolphins appeared. Three of them. Out of the deep. Swimming fast and turning in tight circles around them. Without thinking, he reached out and caught hold of a shining, grey dorsal fin, and kicked for the surface.

'I don't know what gets into you, love. I really don't.'

'Sorry, Mum.'

She was looking disappointed again.

'The doctor says you're to stay in bed and rest,' she said. 'You have swallowed a lot of sea water and it has made you sick.'

'But I feel better now, Mum,' he said.

'No *buts*,' she said, and meant it. 'That's why I told those friends of yours they would have to come back tomorrow.'

'Friends?'

She nodded. 'There was a whole crowd of them round before – I didn't know you had so many.'

Russ was standing at the window looking out over the bay. The outer break which marked Coffin was no more than a distant white line.

'What were you doing all the way out there, anyway?' he asked.

Jim gripped the shell tightly and wondered if he should tell them. But what could he say? That he was a time traveller who had been called into his own future by a ghost of a surfer called Bono. That Bono had given him a seashell. And that a dolphin had just saved his life. How could he expect them to believe all that?

'I lost my board,' he said instead.

'Good job, too,' his mum said, sounding cross. 'Because there's going to be no more surfing for you my lad, and that's final.'

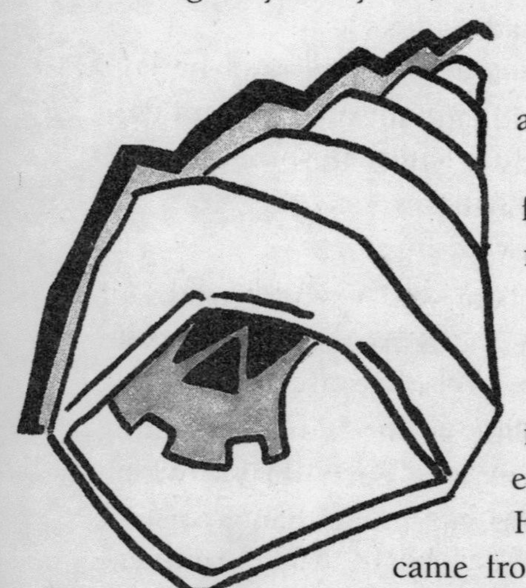

'But Mum!'

'Final,' she said, and walked out.

Jim lay in bed, fingering the shell miserably.

'What you got there, mate?' Russ asked, coming to sit on the end of his bed.

He shrugged. 'It came from the outer reef

– I think it might be valuable or something.'

Russ took the shell and held it up. The light caught on its curves and whorls, gleaming silver and pink. 'It's a Mollusc shell. Probably has had a small hermit crab in it too,' he said. 'Been under water a long time – but it's nothing special.' He tossed it back to Jim. 'Sorry, mate.'

Jim was disappointed.

Spinner's face appeared at the window, nose pressed against the glass. He ducked back down out of sight when he saw Russ.

'I think I feel a bit tired now,' Jim said quickly. He made a big show of yawning and stretching.

Russ told him to get some rest and he lay back, eyes closed. He waited until he heard the door click shut as Russ left, then sprang out of bed and opened the window.

Andy and Tango were arguing.

'No way! Sticks aren't electric,' Andy said.

'Then some dude must be giving off sparkies round this neck, because I'm feeling the vibes, man,' Tango said.

'Shhhhhhh!' Jim hissed. 'My mum'll throw a wobbly if she hears you.'

'We've brought your board back,' Spinner

said. 'Tango found it washed up on the beach.'

Tango nodded. 'Man, is that one full-on, neon honey,' he said, only too pleased to be rid of the board which seemed to be giving off sparks every time he touched it.

They passed it in through the window and Jim quickly hid it under his bed. One by one, they clambered in and flopped down, squabbling over who sat where and who was next with Jim's Gameboy.

Only Finny was missing.

'Finny won't come here,' Sal said.

The others went quiet, as if she had said something she should not have done.

'Why not?' Jim asked.

Spinner's eyes flicked from face to face. 'I think we should tell him.'

Sal nodded, then Tango and finally Andy.

'Tell me what?'

'The Bonningtons owned this house . . .' Spinner started.

'But they moved to Adelaide suddenly,' Sal went on.

'Van moosed,' Tango said.

'Leaving the place empty.' Andy confirmed it beyond all doubt.

'And?' Jim asked with growing frustration.

'Look, we don't believe it,' Spinner said, shaking his head, 'but—'

'But *what*?'

'A few months after they'd gone, Finny came up here,' Spinner said. 'She says she doesn't know what made her come. She just did. That's when she saw him standing at the window – your bedroom window.'

'Saw who?'

'Matthew Bonnington,' Spinner said.

'Who's he?'

'*Was*,' Spinner corrected him. 'Matthew Bonnington was Bono.'

It had been Bono's house. Bono's room. Bono's life, before his. And knowing it left Jim with the strangest feeling. The feeling that somehow he had taken over from where Bono had left off. To finish what had been left unfinished.

As if that wasn't enough to think about – next, a car pulled up outside. Doors slammed. There was a loud knocking on the door. Moments later they heard Mr Grist's voice.

They crowded around the door as Jim opened it a crack, looking down the long passage. Russ had opened the front door and was talking to Mr Grist on the doorstep.

'He's probably come to complain about the coke,' Spinner said.

'Maybe it stained his car,' Sal said.

'Or rotted it away to nothing,' Andy said, 'like it does teeth.'

'Far out!' Tango said.

Images of a melted wreck smouldering in their driveway filled Jim's head. What if he had to pay for it? A car that long would take a million years on his pocket money.

'. . . I'm glad I caught you, Russel,' Mr Grist was saying. 'I wanted a quiet word. He put an arm around Russ's shoulder like a long-lost friend. 'It's a delicate matter so perhaps we can take a walk in the garden, where it's more private . . .'

Their voices faded and Jim's heart sank. 'I'm cat food,' he groaned.

Whatever was said, it was definitely *bad*, because a few minutes later they heard raised voices. Russ came storming back into the house, followed to the door by Mr Grist.

'Don't take it like that, Russel,' Mr Grist called through the flyscreen. 'It's not much to ask. They'll have to believe a marine biologist with a laboratory.'

Russ shook his head. 'But how can I say the water in the bay is clean without testing it?'

'Why worry about little details like that?' Mr Grist said. 'The people round here will be happy to know it's safe to swim. You get a tidy sum to fix up this run-down heap you call a house. My company is cleared. And I get elected on to Whaler's Bay Council. Bingo! Everyone is happy.'

'I can't do it, Mr Grist,' Russ said, shaking his head. 'Sorry.'

The smile died on Mr Grist's lips. He muttered darkly, something about Russ regretting the day he made an enemy of Morgan Grist, then turned his back. Jim breathed a sigh of relief when he heard the car roar away, tyres screeching.

His mum appeared, heading down the passage towards them.

'Hide! Quick!' he said.

Confusion and panic. They ran around in circles looking for places to hide. Sal jumped straight out the window into the bushes. Spinner and Andy squashed into the wardrobe. Tango ended up down the bed. Jim threw the covers over them both and waited for the storm.

'Are you all right, love?' his mum said, poking her head round the door.

He nodded his head until it almost fell off. 'I'm OK!' he blurted. 'Just resting like the doctor said.'

She smiled. 'That's good, love. But maybe your friends should go home now,' she said and closed the door.

One by one they came out of hiding.

'How did she know?' Spinner asked, blinking a lot.

Jim shrugged. 'She's got radar.'

A storm *was* brewing, but it was not the kind Jim was expecting. It was a real storm, the like of which he had never seen. But before the storm, came an eerie calm.

Evening fell early, the light fading to a milky stain on the far horizon. The darkness weighing heavy with the heat.

Jim dosed into a fitful sleep. Tossing and turning, covers thrown off. Only to wake suddenly, feeling a cold hand on his shoulder, shaking him. He sat up, rubbing the sleep from his eyes, expecting to see his mum by his bedside, but his room was empty.

It was just past midnight. The curtains were moving in the faint breeze, moonlight streaming in through the gaps.

'Was that you, Bono?' he whispered.

No answer.

He crept over to the window and looked

out. The moon hung low in the sky, fat and round, like a ball of wax. Below, the bushes and dunes were just lumps of shadow. The sluggish surf washed the sand. Beyond, the sea was like black glass.

The sound of an engine carried on the still night air. The steady chug of a boat. It crossed the line of mirrored light thrown down on the water by the moon, silhouetted for a brief while before being swallowed up by the darkness once more. He heard the engine cut to a low growl.

'It's stopped out near Coffin,' he said.

Something went into the water, *splash!* The anchor? No. The engine was still running. *Splash!* in went another. And another.

A stirring amongst the shadows caught his eye. Someone was moving around the dunes down by the beach, flitting from here to there, careful to stay out of the moonlight.

His heart beat faster, drumming loudly in his chest. Was it Bono? It was hard to tell.

Breathlessly, he pulled on a pair of shorts and scrabbled around on the floor until he found his flashlight. He stamped his feet into his trainers, climbed out of the window and hit the ground running.

The bushes scratched his bare arms and legs with twig fingers as he scrambled down the steep path to the beach. He came to a sliding halt, the beam of light flicking wildly round the dunes.

'Is that you, Jim?' a voice called, making him jump.

'Wh-wh-who?' He only seemed capable of owl impressions.

'The light! Someone will see it!'

'Sorry,' he said, fumbling with the switch. The light died and the shadows crowded in all around, for a while even deeper than before.

'Up here!' the voice said.

A face appeared on the rounded top of a big, bald dune.

'Russ? Is that you?'

'Shh! Sound can travel for miles across water – especially on a still night,' Russ said. 'And come up the back of the dune, that way they won't see you.'

Jim climbed up the shifting sand, crawling the last part of the way until he wriggled up alongside Russ. They spoke in whispers after that.

'What are you doing?' Jim asked.

'Watching.'

'The boat?'

Russ nodded.

From the top of the dune they could see the boat silhouetted against the moon. The skipper was holding her steady just outside the break, stern dangerously close to where the waves were curling. Jim could see figures moving about on deck. Every now and again, something heavy was rolled overboard with a loud splash.

'I think those are metal drums going in,' Russ said.

Splash! In went another.

'But they can't dump them there, can they?' Jim said.

Splash!

'No way, mate!'

'Then shouldn't we report them, or something?'

'Too late,' Russ said. 'They'll be long gone before the coast guard gets here and anyway we don't even know whose boat it is.'

As if to prove him right, the boat's engine coughed, then spluttered into life. Throttled low, it turned slowly in a wide circle and set off towards the town. They watched it slink away until the darkness threw a shroud over it like a guilty secret.

Russ rolled on to his back and looked up at the night sky. Silent, hands folded on his chest, lost in his own thoughts.

Jim copied him and lay staring up at the stars. Australia seemed to have more than anywhere else in the world. Millions and millions, all pure white. Then he noticed the thick clouds piling up on the edge of his world, blotting out the winking points of light one by one.

'Mr Grist came to see me today,' Russ said, breaking the silence. 'I couldn't sleep for thinking about some of the things he said – that's why I came down here to think.'

Jim was on his guard. 'What sort of things?'

'Well, for a start he tried to bribe me,' Russ said. 'And when I told him I wasn't interested in his money he tried to blame you for messing up his limousine. That man will say *anything*.'

'Anything,' Jim said weakly.

Russ sat up abruptly as if an idea had come to him. He glanced out to sea, then back at Jim. 'You've been out to that reef,' he said.

'Yes, but I promised I wouldn't—'

'Don't worry, mate,' Russ interrupted. 'Just tell me why they call it Coffin?'

'Because there's a long hole in the reef,' Jim said, and repeated what Spinner had said about seeing it from the air.

'Of course,' Russ said, more to himself than Jim. 'A crack in the reef. Deep water. Heavy surf running most of the year. It's the perfect place to dump something you don't want to be found. No one goes anywhere near the place except . . .'

'Except surfers,' Jim said, finishing for him.

'Mr Grist said that the surfers had been causing him trouble. Complaining. Saying there were chemicals in the water.'

The more Jim thought about it, the more the pieces of the puzzle began to fit together: Morgan Grist Chemicals, the boat, things being dumped in the middle of the night; and everyone knew Bono had disappeared while surfing Coffin.

'Could they . . . be dangerous – the chemicals, I mean?' he asked.

'That depends on what they are. I would need to run some tests in the lab,' Russ said. 'But it will take time to collect water samples, especially with a storm coming.' He sighed and shook his head. 'If only we had something from the outer reef. Something that's been in the water a long time – anything.'

'Bono's shell! I knew it was important,' Jim said, digging deep into the pocket of his long shorts. 'Would it do?'

'Too right!' Russ said. 'At least it will be good for a start.'

12

The next morning the wind had turned northerly. Hot and dusty, blowing out of the red heart of Australia. The sun came up late, like a giant slice of blood orange, its bright shine dulled but not its heat.

The dust found its way everywhere. Stinging Jim's eyes and crunching between his teeth. Even his underpants felt gritty, making it harder than usual to sit still and concentrate at school.

All day he kept glancing out of the window, wondering what secrets the shell had been keeping. Russ had promised to carry out the tests first thing. It was the *not knowing* which was hardest.

Then, with only five minutes of the final lesson to go, he saw Russ's blue four-wheel-drive pull up. The sight of it parked outside set him bouncing about in his seat. That was when disaster struck in the form of Mr Maddox.

'And perhaps Jim Troon can tell us which giant of the literary scene wrote the play *Romeo and Juliet*?' Mr Maddox said.

Startled, Jim glanced up and found everyone looking at him, expecting an answer. 'Er . . . Well . . . Um . . .' he said.

But it seemed Mr Maddox expected more. 'You weren't listening, were you, Jim?' he said.

Jim assured him he had been hanging on his every word.

A crafty look came into Mr Maddox's eye. 'Then what did I just say?'

'Er, you said . . . I wasn't listening. But I was!'

'*Before* that.'

Jim felt the heat more than ever. He racked his brains, but came up blank. So he turned to his neighbour for help. Unfortunately, it was Tango.

'Maddo's main man,' Tango whispered the answer. 'The dude with the quills and the dumb tights.'

Jim used up a lot of brain cells working it out, but he came up with the answer in the end: 'Big Bird?' he said.

What kept you, mate?' Russ asked, as he slid into the passenger seat of the truck and slammed the door.

'Mr Maddox,' Jim said, moodily. 'He made me stay behind and write out fifty times, "William Shakespeare does not live on Sesame Street." '

'Stratford-upon-Avon, wasn't it?' Russ said, then thoughtfully changed the subject. 'I ran the tests on that shell of yours.'

'It's Bono' shell,' Jim said.

'I'd like to talk to this Bono – is he a mate of yours?'

'Sort of,' Jim said. 'But what about the shell?'

'The tests showed traces of lead, mercury and arsenic.'

'*Arsenic*, but that's poison, isn't it?'

'They all are in one way or another, and they are all used or produced as waste in certain chemical processes.'

'So those drums were full of chemical waste!'

Russ shook his head. 'Not necessarily. I expected higher readings, but I only found tiny traces. And anyway it would be hard to prove that the shell definitely came from the outer reef,' he said. 'The only way we are going to know for sure, is if we test the water.'

Russ had six small bottles in a case on the

floor of his four-wheel-drive. The coloured caps were numbered. They were for holding water samples so he could take them back to the lab for testing. Six bottles for six samples, each to be taken from a different place.

'It's going to be difficult,' Russ said. 'The guys in the surf patrol say it's too dangerous to take a rubber boat into the middle of the surf. And with the storm coming the waves are only going to get bigger.'

Jim picked out one of the little bottles and weighed it in his hand. It was made of tough, lightweight plastic. But despite its wide neck, he could see it would take time to fill properly, especially if the boat was constantly dodging the waves. And there were six of them. *Six.*

That was when he had a wild idea.

'I've got to talk to the others,' he said. 'Can we stop at Sharky's place on the way?'

'You wanna milkshake, kid?' Sharky asked. 'Chocolato? Strawberry? I gotta—'

'Everything, yes I know,' Jim said, 'but I'm only looking for Spinner and the others.'

Sharky rolled his eyes. 'What is it with this kid – he'sa always looking for somebody!' he said to the crow.

The crow flapped its wings and fixed Jim with a beady eye.

Spinner was busy seeing if he could suck the jam out of a doughnut through a striped drinking straw. The others were there. Even Finny.

'I want to call a meeting,' Jim said. 'It's important.'

'So's this,' Spinner said. 'I'm trying for the world record.'

'Ready. Steady. Go!' Andy said, timing him.

Spinner's cheeks caved in and his eyes bulged out. He sucked, straining for all he was worth, making funny squeaking noises.

'What is the world record?' Jim asked, hoping it would not take too long.

Andy shrugged. 'There isn't one – no one has ever tried it before.'

Spinner collapsed in a breathless heap on the table and Andy promptly declared it a 'No jam score.'

'How about me trying to beat the record for eating Lamingtons?' Spinner said hopefully. 'But I've got no money so you'll be paying.'

'We haven't got time to waste on stupid stuff like this,' Jim said, interrupting. He was angry now.

'Stupid, is it?' Spinner said. 'Well, that's good coming from someone who thinks Daffy Duck is a (and here he mimicked Mr Maddox) "giant of the literary scene." '

'I do *not*. Anyway, it was Big Bird,' Jim said, falling into Spinner's trap.

'Big Bird!' they hooted, falling about they laughed so much.

Jim could see he was wasting his time. He stood up, pushing back his chair with a loud scraping noise.

'Something bad is going to happen and you are just going to sit around sucking jam out of doughnuts and let it,' he said. 'No wonder Bono had to call on me for help.'

The part about Bono just slipped out without him meaning it to. But once it was said, he was glad.

'Bono!' they all said at once.

Spinner nudged Tango and grinned.

'I've seen him,' Jim said.

'Oh yeah – so what did he look like?' Spinner asked.

Jim described Bono to them. His dark hair and eyes. The way he looked. The way he stood. And as he spoke the mocking smile died on Spinner's lips.

'How would he know all that if he hadn't seen him?' Andy asked.

'He might have seen a photograph,' Spinner said.

'You have to believe me,' Jim said. 'Bono's here in Whaler's Bay. Tell them, Finny! Even Spinner will have to believe two of us!'

All eyes turned to Finny, but she looked away and said nothing.

'I can see I'm wasting my breath,' Jim said. 'But you'll be sorry. You'll *all* be sorry you didn't listen to me.'

An uneasy quiet descended upon them and he knew they were watching him every step of the way to the door. Outside, Russ was waiting in the four-wheel-drive.

What am I going to do now? Jim thought, thrusting his hands deep into the pockets of his long shorts. He kicked out at a stone and sent it flying.

'Hey, wait!'

He glanced over his shoulder and saw Finny standing in the doorway. 'What do *you* want?' he said.

'Was it true what you just said – about Bono?' she asked in a quiet voice.

'Why should you care?' he said, suspecting a wind-up. But the others were not smirking around the door or crowding around the window, noses pressed against the glass.

She stood twisting her hands in front of her.

'It's just that the others said I was seeing things,' she said. 'They laughed. They made me feel stupid. That's why I didn't say anything just now.'

'But you did see him?'

She nodded. 'It was Bono at that window. He was just standing there, pointing out at the bay. It was so scary.' Her eyes searched his face. 'He's come back, hasn't he – from the dead, I mean.'

'He's trying to tell us something,' Jim said. 'Trying to warn us.'

'Warn us? How do you mean?' she asked, glancing about uneasily as if she half expected to see Bono standing nearby.

Jim told her about the boat and the metal drums. About the tests Russ had carried out in his lab on the shell and how they had shown traces of lead, mercury and arsenic. And how they needed more samples to be sure the chemicals were in the water.

'I think Bono is trying to warn us about the danger,' he said. 'But I need help to find out if there are chemicals in the water for sure. That's why we have to go out to Coffin *now* – before the storm hits.'

Finny looked up at the dark clouds which were packing up in the sky. The gusting wind flicked her hair over her face.

'There was a storm like this just before Bono disappeared,' she said. 'He went out surfing the day after. Reckoned the waves were too good to miss. We never saw him again.' She smiled, but there were tears in her eyes. 'He was always saying he wanted to surf away with the dolphins. Free.'

'Will you help me to persuade the others?' Jim asked. 'For Bono's sake.'

'But what can we do? We haven't got boats,' she said.

Jim shook his head. 'We don't need boats. We need surf boards.'

Finny thought for long while before she spoke. 'You're right,' she said. 'Even Spinner will have to believe two of us.'

13

They could do it, couldn't they? Yes. Jim was definitely sure they could do it. Well, probably definitely, anyway.

They were in the water, out in the deep blue beyond Coffin, sitting astride their boards, riding the swell. Russ was standing by in the rubber boat, the outboard engine *put*, *put*, *putting*. He was ready to come to the rescue if anything went wrong.

Jim cast a wary eye over the waves breaking in front of him. They were big, but not too big, coming in regular sets. More importantly, the off shore wind was holding them up nicely, so they peeled in for an even break. It was as close to calm as Coffin would ever be.

'I still don't believe in ghosts,' Spinner said for the umpteenth time. 'I've only come along because I'm the best big-wave rider in Whaler's.' He laughed, but it sounded hollow.

'The best? Dream on!' Sal said.

'It's ride or die,' Tango said, giving the pinky and thumb salute.

'I wish he'd stop saying that,' Andy said.

Together, Jim and Finny had been able to convince the others. It had not been easy. After all, they were talking *ghosts*. But they came round in the end. Sal and Andy, first. Then Tango. Finally, even Spinner; although he kept saying he was only going along for the ride.

Jim's plan was simple. They would go one by one. Once, and once only. Each choosing their own wave and taking the drop at a different point along the break. That way the samples of water would come from different places.

No messing about. They were to drop deep into the trough, crouch low, and scoop the plastic bottles through the water. Then they were to get out of the impact zone as fast as possible, taking the full bottles back to Russ who would be waiting in the boat.

'We haven't got much time,' Jim said, looking up at the sky. It was ominously dark and he could see the flicker of lightening in the distance.

It had been hard to persuade Russ that they could do it. That a surfer, moving quickly, could go where no boat could. That the waves were ideal. They could be in and out, collecting the samples quickly, and even be home for tea.

'Just don't *ever* tell your mother,' Russ said.

Jim decided to go first. Partly because it had been his idea, and partly because he felt he could not ask the others to do something he had not tried himself. Finny volunteered next. Then Sal. Andy. Tango. Spinner chose to go last.

They lined up and waited.

'Keep chillin'!' 'Stay cool!' 'Rock on!' they called as Jim paddled into position.

He flipped open the lid of the little plastic bottle and clamped it in his teeth. A quick glance over his shoulder and he had picked his wave. It was third in a set of three. He waited patiently for the first and second to roll under him, then turned to make his run.

I wish Danny could see me now, he thought.

The board seemed to sense his excitement as he powered towards the distant shore. Paddling, arm over arm, knowing he had one chance and one chance only. He could not risk another run if there were dangerous chemicals in the water.

The board bucked beneath him as the wave caught him up. He surged forward in a final spurt and felt the familiar buzz running through the rails. It flowed in him like electric blood. Giving him super-strength and lighting him up until he was sure he glowed like a neon sign. He made the jump.

From peak to trough the wave was not big. No monster at all. It was glassy smooth. Shaded blue and glittering with reflected light. Perfect. Beautiful. And yet he knew it was a beauty the shredder would destroy.

His board shredded down the steep face as he swooped deep into the trough. He let his own momentum take him into the turn. Then he was snatching the bottle out of his mouth, crouching as low as he could, and dipping it into the water. A moment later – the bottle full – he snapped the cap shut with his thumb and punched at the air.

The others whooped and hollered with

excitement, their shouts like seabirds crying on the wind.

With the wave curling in, he cut back up the face hoping to regain speed. But the lip dissolved in front of him and he shot into the air. Somersaulted through a perfect 360 aerial and hit the water hard. Had another wave been following close behind it would have wiped him out.

'I thought I said no fancy stuff,' Russ said, as Jim paddled up.

'Didn't mean to,' he panted. He held out the little bottle and grinned as Russ took it.

By the time Jim had clambered into the rubber boat and pulled his board in after him, Finny was already cutting down the face of the next wave. He watched as she made a smooth, shallow turn and saw her dip the bottle in. She rode the wave out to the shoulder and sank into the froth.

'Easy!' she said, as she paddled up and dropped the little bottle into the bottom of the boat.

Two.

Sal was up next. A goofy – riding her board with her right foot forward – she picked the biggest in a set and carved it up. Fanning the water into sparkles on the turn, dipping and rising, and holding the full bottle high above her head triumphantly. She paddled up to join Finny sitting on her board by the side of the boat. They slapped high-fives.

'*Fat* ace!' Sal said. 'I never knew Coffin was so good.'

Three.

'Look! Dolphins!' Finny said.

Jim followed her gaze and saw them break through the face of the wave. Shining grey. Half fish, half sea-spirits. They skittered and danced across the water playfully, surfing as no human could.

'Where's Andy?' Jim said, shading his eyes.

And suddenly he was filled with a sense of foreboding. As if his plan had been going too smoothly.

Unfortunately, Andy did not see the dolphins until he came over the top. The surprise was total. No one could blame him for losing his line. The sight of three big fish scalloping the wave in smooth curves would have been enough to bring down the best.

They watched as he tried for the turn. It was too sharp. The rail dug in and he climbed right through the curl and slipped out the back-door. He was quick to gather up his board and ducked through the waves which followed.

'I lost my bottle,' he said miserably, when he finally reached the boat.

Three out of four.

Jim tried to shake off the feeling of dread as he watched Tango begin his run.

They heard him whoop excitedly as he came over the lip. He chose the most the radical line possible and cut white water all the way down into the trough. He was totally committed to the wave when disaster struck.

Spinner appeared out of nowhere. Unable, as ever, to wait his turn he had gone for the same wave. He dropped in just as Tango was trying to pull out of his death-defying dive. Tango looked up, too late. Spinner's board sliced down as deadly as a giant blade.

To Jim, watching helplessly, it all happened in slow motion – just like in the movies. Spinner tried for the turn, but caught Tango a glancing blow, flicking him away in a whirl of arms and legs. Spinner waggled his arms as he fought to keep his balance. Cut back, regained momentum and surfed out of the impact zone. Safe.

'Tango!' Jim shouted.

'Hold on!' Russ said, above the roar of the engine as he opened the throttle. 'We're going in.'

They let the next wave pass, then Jim felt the nose of the rubber boat lift as they went in fast. They bumped across the water, the salt spray stinging their faces.

'Tan-go! Tan-go!' they called, over and over.

'We've only got time for one turn,' Russ said, the wind whipping his hair about.

Already the next wave was rising up from the deep.

Russ cut the engine and they slowed into a sweeping turn. They stood up as best they could, steadying one another as they scanned the water for any sign of Tango.

'Is that him?' Jim said.

It was Tango all right. He was lying in the water, dangerously close to the oncoming wave. Russ opened the throttle, and they were off again, bouncing across the chop.

Jim knew they were going up and over long before Russ told him to hold on tight. It was not the biggest wave he had ever seen, but even so they seemed to rise up its face forever. Up towards the brooding sky. Up to nothingness. The outboard screamed as the propeller came out of the water. They hung in the air for what seemed an age, then down they came with a jolt which rattled the teeth in Jim's head and left his stomach far behind.

Again, Russ cut the engine. Again, they scanned the water for Tango.

'There!' Jim said, pointing.

This time they managed to bring the boat alongside Tango as he floated on his board.

'You OK, mate?' Russ said, lifting him out of the water by the seat of his shorts.

Tango slithered into the bottom of the boat gasping like a stranded fish. He showed Jim the full bottle he had clutched firmly in his fist.

Four out of six.

'Geeze, man,' Tango said, grinning fit to bust. 'I never wiped out so *bad*.'

Jim laughed. In Tango-speak that meant good.

By dusk the wind had lost its senses. Blowing up great gusts which flattened the sedge grass and made the house shake and shudder. Jim helped Russ tie the metal sheets of the roof down with thick ropes. The lightening flickered all round, stabbing down in crooked forks, as if some giant goblin had the world on his plate. Then came the rain. Hard as bolts rattling on the roof.

The storm raged all the next day and into a second night. Moulding mountains in the sea and whisking the surf white. Jim watched plumes of foaming spume puff off the crests, jinking in the air, as fragile as paper kites, until the wind spiralled them away. And all the while the waves rolled in like road-trains, smashing on the rocks and scooping hollows in the sand.

Often waking, Jim once thought he saw Bono standing at the window. Tears wet on his cheeks. But when the lightning flickered no one was there.

At last storm blew itself out. The sun returned. Fresh. The breeze cooler. And once again, Jim woke to the warbling calls of the magpies.

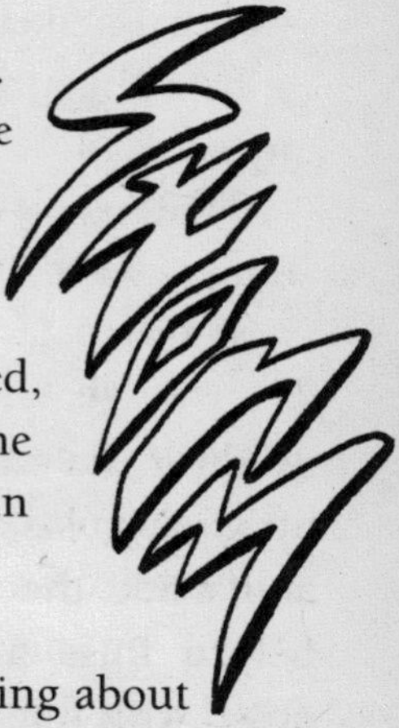

'Those friends of yours called, love,' his mum said, drawing the curtains and letting the sun stream in.

He sat up in bed. 'When?'

'Just now. Fiona Finn was asking about some tests. I haven't got a clue what that Tango was saying. Something about wanting to cruise the all-time post-storm fizz, whatever that means,' she said, with a sigh and a shake of her head. 'I told them it was too early and that they should come back later – so I suppose they'll be round to your window in a minute.'

Sure enough, as soon as she left the room, Jim saw Spinner's nose pressed up against the smeary glass. They were arguing again when he opened the window to let them in:

'. . . My wave was as a big as this house,' Sal was saying.

Andy shook his head. 'Mine must have been bigger for all those dolphins to fit in it

– so that makes me the best.'

'Best at getting pearled and hammered!' Spinner said.

'That's good coming from the kook who stole Tango's wave,' Finny said.

Spinner's face flushed an angry red. 'It was big enough for two,' he said. 'Which just goes to show mine was the biggest of the lot.'

'It was full-on biscuitsville*, man,' Tango muttered, chuckling to himself.

One by one they clambered in, making the usual fuss. Only Finny hesitated.

'It's OK,' Jim said, holding out his hand. 'Bono would never hurt you, especially now we've done what he wanted us to do.'

They settled and looked to Jim for news. Russ had promised the results of his tests as soon as possible, and it could not be soon enough for them. The surf was really pumping after the storm. The diehards would be out first, then others. People would have to be told if it was not safe.

'Hey, maybe we should call Mr Morgan Grist anyway,' Spinner said. 'Tell him we know he's been dumping chemicals. Tell him he's not going to get away with it.'

No sooner had the idea been suggested, than

it was being done. Andy found Mr Grist's home telephone number in the directory and Sal made the call. She was especially pleased when she woke Mr Grist up.

'. . . so we'll have all the proof we need when Russ comes back with the results of the tests,' she said, finally.

Spinner snatched the telephone away from her ear, 'And we are going to run you out of town,' he said, sounding just like a sheriff in an old Western.

'You're previous, man. *Previous*,' Tango added for good measure.

They barely had time to put down the telephone, before Mr Grist was hammering at the door.

'I hope you're writing all this down, Ms Pender,' Mr Grist said. 'This is blackmail.'

'B-la-ck-ma-il,' Ms Pender repeated, her pencil scratching on her note-pad.

She was as neatly dressed as ever.

Mr Grist, on the other hand, had the crumpled look of someone who had come straight from his bed. His striped pyjamas showed under his coat and his hair was sticking up. He constantly scratched at the bristles which shaded his chin.

'What have you done, love?' Jim's mum asked, her radar turned up full.

'I'll tell you what the little *loves* have done,' Mr Grist said, prowling around the kitchen. 'They've dragged me out of bed. Accused me – an upstanding citizen and soon to be elected councillor – of letting my company dump chemicals in the bay. Then tried to blackmail me into leaving Whaler's Bay for good.' He sucked air over his teeth and shook his head. 'Just wait until I tell the police about this.'

'They ought to be locked up,' Ms Pender agreed.

'And where's Russel while all this is going on?' Mr Grist asked.

'He went out early,' Jim's mum said. 'But he'll be back soon.'

Jim wished Russ would hurry. They needed the results of those tests, and they needed them fast. The situation was turning nastier by the minute.

'What did I tell you, Ms Pender,' Mr Grist said, smirking. 'They haven't got any samples. They haven't got any proof.'

'I knew it,' Ms Pender muttered. 'I knew Captain Moody would never have said anything about using the Seabell to—'

'THANK YOU! Ms Pender,' Mr Grist snarled, teeth clenched. His face was suddenly very grey despite his sun-tan. 'I don't think we need to mention any more about *that*.'

They all heard Russ's four-wheel-drive pull up, tyres crunching, and crowded to the door in a scrum. Russ looked surprised to see them all piling out, especially Mr Grist.

'These young hooligans say you have been doing tests on the outer reef,' Mr Grist said, pushing his way to the front of the crowd. 'Well, is it true?'

'Yes,' Russ said, 'I've run some tests.'

'Go on, tell him, Russ,' Jim said. 'Tell him about the lead and mercury and arsenic in the water. Tell him he's been polluting the sea . . .' His voice trailed away when Russ shook his head.

'You shouldn't have said anything. Not until we knew for sure,' Russ said, sounding cross. 'Because those tests – they were all negative.'

Jim stared at him. '*Negative!* But that means . . .'

'Too right it does,' Mr Grist said, regaining his composure suddenly. 'It means you lot are going to be hearing from my lawyers. And by the time I've finished with you, you'll wish you had never heard of the name Morgan Grist.'

'It's all my fault. I thought Bono was trying to warn us,' Jim said. 'I was wrong. Spinner was right. I must have imagined it all. After all, ghosts don't exist, do they?'

Finny sighed and supposed not. Then, after a pause, she said, 'At least we know there aren't any chemicals in the water. So that puts Mr Grist in the clear.'

Jim picked up his board and they walked along the water's edge, stopping once in a while to look at the sea things which lay strewn about on the polished sand: sea urchins, jellyfish, weed which popped under their toes, coloured kelp, and cuttlefish; fan-shaped shells with broken edges; whelks and cockles and spindles. All cast upon the shore like little gifts from a repentant sea.

'Bono loved the time after the storms best,' Finny said, looking out over the waves. 'He said the sea was at its best just after the rage had gone out of it.'

The wind had dropped and, even though the sea was still running after the storm, the waves were peeling nicely. Jim could see the others picking up regular sets. He could hear their shouts as they wave-larked about, zig-zagging, cruising, shredding the surf to foam.

'Think I'll catch some too – now I know it's safe,' Finny said. 'Waves like that are too good to miss.'

Jim watched as she knelt to strap the plastic leash to her ankle then splashed out into the backwash.

And suddenly he was angry.

'Why am I here?' he shouted into the roar and hiss of the waves. 'Is it all a big joke?' He picked up a spiny Murex shell and hurled it into the sea.

And after anger, came despair. He threw his board on to the sand and sat down. The tears welling up in his eyes as he buried his face in his hands.

'It's not that bad, mate,' he heard Russ say.

He rubbed the tears away quickly as Russ sat down beside him.

'Your mum's not too pleased with either of

us,' Russ said. 'But at least Mr Grist has promised not to set his lawyers on us if I send the results of my tests to the *Whaler's Bay Advertiser*.' He smiled wryly. 'The old shark got what he wanted all along – people like that always do.'

'But what about the boat?' Jim asked.

'Who knows,' Russ said, 'it could have been a fishing boat dropping off lobster pots – anything.' He paused, thought for a moment, then frowned. 'Mind you, they don't usually put out pots just before a big storm.'

Jim looked up. 'Why not?'

'Because when the sea gets stirred up it can do a lot of damage,' Russ said. 'A fisherman could lose the lot – and those pots are expensive.'

'Would it get stirred up right down to the bottom – even out at Coffin?' Jim asked.

Russ nodded. 'Sure would. A big storm like that can do a lot of damage, especially on a shallow reef.'

Jim looked out over the waves. A bag of surfers had split away from the main pack. He stood up to see better, shading his eyes with his hand.

Was that Spinner and Tango? Yes. He was

sure of it. Sal and Andy, too. He could see Finny waving to them, calling. Then she dropped out of the line-up and started paddling after them.

'They are heading for Coffin,' he said.

Just as Bono had done, they were going out to surf Coffin after a storm. A storm which had stirred the sea to a seething frenzy. And as Jim watched his friends, he knew they would not be going had he not shown them the way.

A terrible thought popped into his head and he turned to Russ. 'Could a storm crack open metal drums?' he asked.

'Easily,' Russ said. 'If they weren't too deep.'

Jim began to feel sick. 'What would happen if the chemicals leaked out?'

'That depends. The waves would disperse them so they wouldn't be that concentrated,' Russ said. 'Unless they were contained somehow – maybe in a hole in the reef . . .'

And suddenly it all began to make sense. Everything. The metal drums *were* in the water, but the chemicals had not leaked out recently. That's why the tests on the water samples had proved negative. The shell, on the other hand, had been in the water longer – when the last leak had turned

Coffin into a death trap.

'The storm,' Jim whispered. 'Bono was trying to warn us about the *storm*.'

'Who is this Bono you're always talking about?' Russ said.

'He's a ghost,' Jim said, snatching up his board.

'What do you mean a *ghost*?' Russ said, startled. 'And where are you going?'

'I'll tell you later,' Jim said. 'The others are in danger. I've got to stop them. Now!'

He ran to the water's edge and, without stopping to attach the board to his ankle, hurled himself into the surf.

Jim paddled as he as he had never paddled before. Thrashing the water to froth. Cutting through the chop. Gasping. Choking. Arm over arm. The board buzzing beneath him. Hardly noticing the waves as he ducked through them, bobbing up on the other side to thrash the water once more.

He paused, once only. Briefly. Just long enough to catch his breath and pick the best line out to Coffin. He caught a glimpse of his friends in the water. They were out beyond the break. Lined up. Spinner, Tango, Andy, and

Sal, sitting on their boards, rising and falling with the swell, waiting for Finny to join them.

Then he saw the crow circling above their heads. An omen. It fluttered, just a black mark against the sky. Marking their doom.

'No! Please! Don't do—' he shouted, but the water slopped into his mouth and choked his words away.

He kicked on, carelessly sacrificing himself to the waves as they rolled in one after the other. His desperation giving him strength. Time after time he was swept back, towards the shore in the seething wash. Only to fight his way out again. Arms and legs aching. His breath coming in ragged gasps.

But nature was too strong for him.

When he saw the wave coming he knew he did not have the strength to duck through it. Scarred and snarling like a champion wrestler, it lifted him up, flipped him over backwards, and hurled him down. Then dropped on him with its full weight in a final devastating smash.

He went down fast and the board was plucked from his grasp. It speared away through the water, as sleek and as graceful as a great, glowing fish. He reached out to catch it, but it was too slippery and smooth. Too quick.

Then the trailing line of the plastic leash cut across his chest and he snatched at it. It slithered through his fingers until he caught hold of the Velcro straps on the end and held on.

Was it a second? An hour? A year? He could not tell. Time had no meaning as the board dragged him through the water. Was he going down, or up? It did not seem important.

And as he looked on helplessly, he saw the board glowing with a strange light. It began to disappear, from its nose down to its tail, until eventually it was gone completely. Then, like a lit fuse, the plastic leash began to vanish in his fingers. He watched as it took his hand and arm, too. All around the water was exploding with colour. Blue turned to silver, then green as he broke the surface, shooting up into the grey of a September day at Wrecker's.

'Told you that board wouldn't work,' Danny said, appearing in front of him.

'Danny! It's you!'

'Course it's me.'

'Then I'm back – I'm home!'

'What are you talking about? And why aren't you wearing anything?'

Jim just laughed as the waves washed him up on to the beach at Wrecker's like a piece of driftwood. He sat up in the shallows, hardly noticing the freezing cold as he splashed about. His board had vanished and he was naked again, but he didn't care. He was home.

Then he looked out at the waves and remembered Finny, Spinner, Tango and the others. And the joy of being home faded. Suddenly he went cold. Deathly cold.

'I couldn't reach them,' he said. 'I couldn't warn them. They're still out there!'

'Who? Out where?' Danny said, looking out at Wrecker's.

The breath caught in Jim's throat. 'I failed,' he sobbed.

16

'The removal van is here, love,' his mum said, poking her head round his bedroom door. 'The men want to pack up our stuff for shipping.'

Jim sat on his suitcase and looked out of the window. Out over Covin Bay towards the rocks of Gunver Point. The sun was dodging in and out of the clouds as they went skudding across the sky. He did not want to leave. Not now.

'Can I go down to Wrecker's?' he asked. 'Danny said he would be there and I want to say goodbye.'

'Well, don't be too long – we have to go soon,' she said, then studied his face and frowned. 'If I didn't know better, I would swear you've managed to get yourself a sun-tan overnight.'

Jim slipped away quickly. His bike had

already been packed away in the big box van so he had to go on foot, cutting across the fields and down to Wrecker's.

Danny was on the beach watching Sean riding the waves. He was sitting inside a circle scratched in the damp sand with Big Mungo rumbling ominously nearby. It seemed Big Mungo wasn't too happy about being bald.

'Sean's getting me back for all the trouble over the Twisted Cat,' he explained. 'Says he might let me out next year sometime – so maybe I'll be able to come and visit you then.'

'Maybe if Gunver turns up again, he could make another board,' Jim said.

'No way! I'll fly in an aeroplane like everyone else,' Danny said. 'Anyway, Sean says Gunver has gone for good.'

Jim looked out towards Gunver point half-hoping he would see Gunver's crimson coat on the skyline.

'We'll be friends forever, won't we?' Jim said, without looking at Danny. 'It doesn't matter where we are.'

'F'rever.'

They slapped hands on it.

'I've got to go now,' Jim said.

He felt as if he had rocks inside him as he

made his way slowly back home. He was already missing Danny and Wrecker's and Porth Covin. Everything. And he had not even left yet. He swore he would come back one day. 'On a dog's head.'

As he turned the corner of his street, he was surprised to see someone wearing a long, crimson coat sitting perched on their gatepost. A crow fluttered uneasily on his shoulder.

'Gunver!' Jim said, breaking into a run. 'You're back. I came looking for you. To tell you. It worked – the board. It actually flew through time.'

Gunver just nodded. That's all. Just nodded, as if he already knew. 'Quite a time you've had by the sound of it, Jim Troon,' he said.

Jim frowned. 'I haven't told anyone 'cept Danny and I can tell he doesn't really believe me,' he said. 'So how did you know?'

Gunver just smiled and stroked the crow under the chin.

'The crow!' Jim said.

Startled, the crow flapped and settled again, fixing him with a beady eye.

'We've got something for you,' Gunver said, reaching inside his coat. He pulled out the broken tip of the surf board.

'Where did you find it?'

'Washed up.'

'Is it all right? Can you fix it? Can you make another board so I can go back?'

The questions blurted out of him as he took the piece of broken plastic and clutched it to his chest. But his voice trailed away when the familiar buzz did not run through him. It felt lifeless. Dead.

'The power has gone out of it,' Gunver said finally. 'It'll not work again.'

Jim sagged as if the disappointment was too much for him to bear. 'Then I really did fail,' he said.

Gunver jumped down from his gatepost in a flap of coat-tails. He clapped a big knuckled hand on Jim's shoulder and looked into his eyes.

'You can't change the past, Jim Troon,' he said. 'You can only make the future better.'

And with that he walked away without looking back.

Jim watched until Gunver turned the corner. Then, clutching the broken board, he walked up the path to his front door. He stood back to let the kitchen table pass, carried by two men in blue overalls, and found himself thinking about what Gunver had said.

'Only make the future better,' he repeated, and his excitement grew. 'The *future*. That's it! I haven't even been to Whaler's Bay yet. There hasn't even been a storm! So I've still got time.'

The sun was hot on his back and neck as Jim knelt to plant the broken nose of a surf-board in the white sand. It leaned short-shadowed and slanting, a plastic gravestone in the mid-day sun. Bono's name was spray-painted across the twisting patterns.

'We miss you, Bono,' Finny said.

Sal nodded. 'Every day.'

'You were the best,' Andy said.

'Apart from me,' Spinner said, unable to wait his turn. 'But we got Mr Grist for you! He won't be dumping any more chemicals in our sea.'

Tango raised his fist in a salute. 'Let surf angels on honeys guide you, man.'

Jim shaded his eyes as he looked out to sea. A school of dolphin were cruising the bay, dipping through the water and surfing on the waves.

Was it his imagination or did he really catch a glimpse of a boy, about his age, out there with them. Surfing. Free.

Glossary

ankle rope – sometimes called leash. Plastic cord which attaches the surfboard to surfer's ankle.
bag of surfers – group
biscuitsville – dunked, wiped out.
blank board – fibreglass block from which new board is carved and painted
break – where the waves begin to curl
buttered board – surfers wax or butter their boards for grip
deck – the flat of the board
dog's head – a sacred oath
drop – as in 'take the drop', surf down the face of a wave
face – smoothest part of the wave
fat – good
fat ace – excellent
grommet – an inexperienced surfer
honey – surfboard
impact zone – where the waves break hardest (to be avoided)
kook – surfer who jumps in and out of waves (insulting)
Lamingtons – type of sticky cake covered in coconut
lip – top of wave
line-up – waiting zone just beyond the break
peak – highest part of wave
peeling – a good wave, as in 'peeling nicely'

pinky and thumb salute – three fingers clenched in a fist with thumb and little finger extended, means 'keep chilling'
plastic leash – *see* ankle rope
pocket – the part of a wave, near the trough, closest to the point where it is curling
pumping – good surf, as in 'surf's pumping'
rail – edge of board
road-trains – huge multi-trailered trucks
sets – waves come in groups, as in 'sets of three'
shoulder – part of the wave furthest away from the peak
Shaper – person who makes boards
skins – naked, bare
stick – surfboard
Surf Shack – name of a shop
sweet spot – smoothest point on the wave where the surfer can go fastest
tapped in – connected, in harmony
Tiger – deadly Australian snake (to be avoided)
trough – bottom of wave
tube – also known as barrel, curling wave you can surf through (best sort of wave)
wipe out – being dumped by wave
Van moosed – Tango's version of vamoose, US slang meaning to leave hurriedly, from Spanish *vamos* meaning 'let's go'
Vets – the veterans who surf the Twisted Cat